*This book is dedicated to ancestors who kept the faith
and who through their own divided loyalties instigated
my growth of compassion and curiosity.*

INCOGNITO
Journey of a Secret Jew

Other works by
María Espinosa:

Novels:

Longing

Dark Plums

Poetry:

Night Music

Love Feelings

Translation/Introduction

Lélia

by George Sand

To Nikki & Tim

INCOGNITO

Journey of a Secret Jew

*with wonderful memories
of Melaque — until
next year !*

a novel by

María Espinosa

*Maria Espinosa
1/7/04*

*I am so glad to
have met you both —*

San Antonio, Texas
2002

Incognito: Journey of a Secret Jew © 2002
by Maria Espinosa

Cover illustration, "Young Woman Reading a Letter"
by Jan Vermeer (1666), used by permission of the
Rijksmuseum, Amsterdam

First Edition

ISBN: 0-930324-79-X (paperback)
ISBN: 0-930324-85-4 (hardcover edition)

Wings Press
627 E. Guenther
San Antonio, Texas 78210
Phone/fax: (210) 271-7805

On-line catalogue and ordering:
www.wingspress.com

St. Philip's College (San Antonio, TX) Cataloging In Publication

Espinosa, Maria
    Incognito: journey of a secret Jew / Maria Espinosa.

190 p. ; 14 cm.
ISBN 0-930324-85-4 (hc)
ISBN 0-930324-79-X (pbk.)

1. Inquisition—Spain—Fiction. 2. Jews—Spain—Fiction.
3. Jews—Migrations –Fiction. 4. Latina–Fiction. I. Title.
II. Glossary.

PS3555.S545 I52 2002
813—dc21

Contents

INCOGNITO

Journey of a Secret Jew

PROLOGUE
Amsterdam, 1507

Soft hands stroked his face.

Footsteps sounded against the tile floor. As Alfonso lay beneath the eiderdown, half delirious with pain, images out of his past rose up.

Wind blew through the open shutters, bringing with it the smell of sea air and noises of people below.

Emilia!

Sometimes grief overwhelmed him, like dark rushing water. There was an emptiness where she used to be.

Although he was sweating, he was chilled down to his bones. The odors of camphor, medicines, and cabbage soup assailed him.

Warm hands changed the dressings around his genitals and applied salve to the wound of his circumcision. These hands smoothed bedclothes, emptied the chamberpot, and fed him spoonfuls of soup. The kind women who attended him seemed like shadows, although they were as substantial as yeasty bread. They spoke in Flemish, a language as thick and coarse as their food, and the soft slushings of their voices vibrated through him.

Emilia hovered invisibly, a mocking smile on her lips. But then her expression changed, and she wept over their infant son as she tried in vain to suckle him. Her breasts were dry of milk.

Sometimes he felt as if he had already died and were living a pale after-life. The Kabbala taught that there was more than one world, and he himself had experienced this.

He longed for the sunlight and the shimmering sea of Cádiz.

CHAPTER 1

Cádiz, 1492

He had been seven years old when the Jews left Spain. On a hot, dry day in late July, thousands of them began to swarm into the city of Cádiz, choking the dusty roads as they made their way towards the port. At times a group would be singing. Some blew trumpets and played timbrels. And sometimes younger ones danced. But most of them simply looked worn and exhausted, their faces and bodies covered with grime. They carried crying babies in their weary arms. Swollen feet were wrapped in rags. The more fortunate rode pack mules or wagons.

Alfonso Valdez de Echevaría watched the Jews from a balcony of his family's house, along with other members of the household. Fascinated by this extraordinary spectacle, he had watched since the church bells rang Lauds at dawn. A tall girl dressed in scarlet led a group of other young girls in a whirling dance. Their bright skirts flared and their long hair billowed out, as they moved to the beat of drums and the ringing of timbrels. An old man collapsed on the ground. Two younger men came to his rescue. One supported his head, while the other held a flask of precious water to his lips.

For months now the child Alfonso had listened to Father Bernardo rage against these Jews in his sermons. The priest rejoiced at their imminent departure. He preached that these people had burrowed like worms into the soul of Spain, as if it were a fresh, firm apple. In a voice ringing with emotion, Father Bernardo spoke of *limpieza*, or cleanliness of blood. Now at last Spain would be pure.

"Why are Jews evil?" Alfonso asked his nursemaid, a girl with long black braids.

"They kill children and crucify them," she said. "As Our Lord was crucified."

"The men have monkeys' tails, and they bleed like women," said a stableman, leering down at the child.

"Oh hush!" cried the nursemaid, blushing.

"Some have cloven hoofs."

"*Sanctu Jésu.* They are the devil's people."

"They're money lenders and thieves, and they're as sly as foxes," said an older male servant who had run up considerable gambling debts.

"Poor wretches," murmured a laundress.

Alfonso looked down at a boy his own size who was kicking the dust as he trudged along, and he wondered if the other child concealed a monkey's tail inside his baggy breeches.

Alfonso's mother, Doña Luisa, had a headache that throbbed as if the Devil himself were plaguing her. She felt faint from the heat, and perspiration soaked her silk dress beneath the armpits. She wished she could give water to these wretched Jews, but trying to assuage their thirst would be like trying to irrigate a desert with water from a dipper. The servants' remarks to her son distressed her. However, she did not think it prudent to intervene. Her own fear wound so tightly inside that she felt as if she were choking. The fear was always with her, lying in wait like a coiled snake. Over the years, authorities within the Church had created such an atmosphere that a mere word, the omission of a prayer, a thoughtless remark could arouse suspicion.

From the church below came the sound of bells ringing Sext, for noon hour prayers. In a little while she would take her place at the dining table. But first she would lie down with some dried lavender blossoms to soothe her aching forehead. Before going inside to the cool darkness of her room, she moved closer to her youngest child, Alfonso, and caressed his soft hair. He could feel the slight pressure of her thighs beneath the silken fabric of her dress on his bare neck. "Mary, Mother of God, have mercy on us sinners," she murmured. "Blessed art thou, and blessed is the fruit of thy womb."

For days the Jews inundated the city, sleeping in streets and plazas, drinking from public wells. The townsfolk finally posted guards at many of them, fearful they would run dry, or worse, that the accursed Jews would poison the water. So desperate were they for food that they might sell a mule or a silver heirloom for a basket of grapes or oranges or a loaf of bread, as if this small amount of nourishment could stave off death.

Alfonso's father, Don Carlos Valdez, had inherited a fleet of trading ships from his father and his father's father. These ships sailed throughout the civilized world. They brought in silks and spices from the Orient, fine leather from Morocco, rosewood from India. They carried oranges and almonds, olive oil, wine, and grains to the Low Countries, gold to Constantinople, silver and jewels to Salonika, fine woven cloth to Palestine.

He had outfitted all his available ships for passengers, and now, overcoming Doña Luisa's objections that Alfonso was too young, Don Carlos insisted that the child see what was going on with his own eyes. So one afternoon Alfonso, in the company of his brothers, went down to the Port.

The streets were less crowded than they had been, as many Jews had already left on ships. Their carriage jolted over the cobblestones. Miguel, who was eleven, sat in front with the driver, joking and spitting out olive pits. Inside the carriage, Rafael was reading from Seneca. Alfonso leaned over his oldest brother's shoulder and tried to make sense of the strange Latin letters on thin paper. He felt an affinity with Rafael, who was large both in body and spirit, gentle, and scholarly, while he was wary of Miguel. At fifteen, Rafael sprouted a small growth of beard and had begun to assist his father in the family shipping business.

"What does it say?" asked Alfonso

"The wise man does not fear death, because none escape it. *Homo sapiente est tranquilus contra mort*," said his older brother. As they approached the harbor, not a breath of wind stirred, although it usually had risen by this time of day. Scarcely a ripple broke the sea's calm surface. Beyond the harbor, crowded with tall-masted sailing vessels, rose limestone cliffs.

The docks were overflowing with Jews. Some were praying. Others huddled together waiting. Still others lay on the ground, weak and barely conscious. Old people gazed into space. Many had sewn yellow stars onto their dark garments, as certain provinces decreed they must. The stench of human waste mingled with smells of the salt sea and tar.

There was a feeling of despair. Many had believed their rabbis who told them to expect a miracle. When they first reached the Port they had shouted with joy and blown trumpets. Then for hours they stared as if bewitched at the gleaming ocean, waiting in vain for the waters to part, as the Red Sea had parted long ago. But they waited in vain. Half dead with hunger and thirst, they watched gentle ripples lap the ships which strained at anchor.

It was not mere chance, said their rabbis, that the final day set for their departure fell on the ninth of Av. On this day the Temple had been destroyed. They had sinned. Only through prayer and faith could they be saved, said the rabbis. But doubt and disillusionment now weakened their faith.

Don Carlos' ships, crammed with Jews, had already sailed for Constantinople. However, he had purchased extra provisions and this food he had loaded onto wagons and instructed his servants to give out freely to those still awaiting passage. Jews swarmed around these wagons. They devoured loaves of bread, figs, oranges, dried sardines, onions, and cheese. They drank from goatskins which held wine and water.

"They're like greedy rats", said Miguel.

"They're starving," said Rafael.

Alfonso tried to see the shape of men's tails beneath their

breeches. He wondered if the Jews truly did crucify children. How then could they pray so fervently? Why would his father give them food?

On the ground a mother and children lay sleeping, all huddled together. Flies buzzed around them, One of the children, a little boy of about three, stirred, rubbed his eyes, then opened them and stared vacantly. His eyes were clouded over with a milky substance. Just then, his father, coming from the wagons with food, took the child in his arms and gently tried to feed him a morsel of orange.

A man with dark skin and unkept hair rocked back and forth as he chanted from a parchment scroll. His eyes were brilliant, and his face glowed with ecstasy, as if he were far away. People gathered around him and joined in the prayers, swaying back and forth in rhythm. Then a woman began to sing. Her voice rose above theirs, pure and strong. The melody was haunting, but almost unbearably sad to Alfonso.

Miguel skimmed a small white stone into the water. He threw a second stone into the midst of the singers, laughing as they scattered in fright. Miguel had an intense, triangular face and was smaller in build than Rafael.

Rafael's face reddened in anger, and he grabbed Miguel's hands, unclenching the fists, prying loose yet another stone. Miguel's lips compressed with emotion. More than once Rafael, when roused from his usual calm state, had given him a sound thrashing.

"Don't!" said Rafael."

"I was only playing."

"They're not dogs."

"They're the Devil's people. So the priests say." Miguel's face took on a half-mocking expression, then grew serious. He kicked restlessly at a stone and suddenly broke into a run. "Catch me if you can, Alfonso!" he shouted. And he began running through the crowds.

Restless himself and eager for movement, Alfonso pursued. Faster and faster he ran, until he felt like a bird ready to soar, but his brother kept receding, until finally he was no longer in view. Alfonso kept running, then skipping, walking, running again, past pack donkeys and mules and men with huge bundles on their backs. He followed a zig zag path of black stones that formed a pattern along the gray cobble-stones.

A bony hand gripped his wrist. "Benji, you've come back from the dead!"

He looked up into the face of an old man with anguished eyes.

"I'm not Benji!" he shouted, trying to pull away, but the old man only gripped harder.

"You look like Benji, my grandson. He was your age. We left him for the vultures, with only a few handfuls of dirt piled over him. We had no time to bury him."

The old man's strong, sour breath enveloped Alfonso. When he looked down, he saw that the man's toenails were blackened and that his sandals were bound to his feet with rags.

The old man whispered in his ear, wetting it with spittle. "You may be dressed like a little *hidalgo* in your fine linen, but our blood runs in your veins. You will be my Benji." Tears streamed down the old man's face and into his dirty grey-white beard.

Alfonso struggled in vain to free himself from the other's grip, as the old man tried to drag him in the direction of a ship which Jews were boarding. Finally, Alfonso kicked him as hard as he could with his leather boot. The old man moaned and doubled over in pain, letting go. Alfonso took off as fast as he could. Nowhere were his brothers in sight, nor could he find his father's wagons or the carriage.

He stumbled over something. When he bent down, he saw it was a woman, her ragged skirt pulled up over her swollen knees. Her eyes stared unblinking at the sky. In panic, he ran faster.

He ran and ran.

Friars in black Domingan robes were wandering among the crowds. They carried wooden crosses, flasks of holy water, loaves of fresh baked bread. They offered Jews a reprieve from exile if they would accept Christ as their Savior. But most paid them no heed. Some turned away and muttered curses under their breath.

Alfonso's side ached, and he was panting for breath, but he dared not stop running. In his fear, he prayed to Jesus, sweet Jesus, whose crucifix hung over his bed and to whom he prayed each night. But this time something happened that he had never experienced before. The golden cross on its thin chain around his neck began to burn his skin. And something outside himself began to guide his steps, making him surefooted and light.

A tall friar was standing over a Jewess who hugged his black-robed knees as she rocked against him. From a distance it looked as if she were engaged in a sexual embrace, but nestled between her body and the priest's robes lay her child, hidden from exposure.

A crowd of Jews was cursing and jeering at her.

The friar, robust as an oak tree, surveyed them with a wintry face, barely able to contain his anger. "Do you accept the Lord as your Saviour?" he asked her.

"Yes, I do, Señor," she murmured. "Oh Señor, I accept the Lord to save my baby. She will die if we do not rest here."

The friar sprinkled holy water from his flask onto her upturned face. As he was pronouncing the words of baptism, a stone whizzed through the air, grazing her ear. Blood trickled onto her shawl. She huddled over the infant to shield it, as another stone flew through the air, hitting the woman, and she crumpled to the ground.

The Jews hooted with rage, while the friar, a stalwart soldier of God, shook his fist at the crowd.

A whip lashed out. Then Alfonso saw his father, Don Carlos Valdez, in a vest of armor astride his black stallion The horse reared up. His father's whip snaked through the air, as he circled the woman and friar, guarding them.

Two Jewish men tried to drag the woman away, and Don
Carlos slashed out once again with his whip. One of the Jews
howled. The flesh of his thumb had been stripped to white
bone, and it hung in shreds. At a signal from Don Carlos, three
of his guards approached on foot and led her away, huddled
like a bird over her child, while Jews and Christians alike
watched with anger.

Alfonso rode back in the carriage with the Jewess and her
child. Miguel and Rafael would return later on horseback.
The child wouldn't stop crying. The woman held it against her,
rocking in rhythm with the jolting motion of the carriage.
Alfonso looked away when she opened her bodice, revealing a
grey, once-white, underblouse, and pushed the child's mouth
gently against her nipple. Then he looked towards her again.
He had seen sheep suckling in the countryside. He had seen
kittens suckling their cat as she lay stretched out on her side in
the shadows of the courtyard, and he had seen a foal suckling
its mother in their stable. Also he had seen women on the
streets and in the market and in plazas suckling the babies
they carried in their shawls. But he had never been so close. If
he reached out, he, too, could touch that breast, which was
soft and milky white in contrast to the leathery tan of her face
and arms.

The woman's dress was of dark material, patched with
newer cloth. Her hair was covered with a blue kerchief, and
she wore delicate filigreed golden earrings. The child suckled
hungrily, while the woman gazed at it in total absorption. She
had a sweet, gentle expression.

The child was puny, red-faced, ugly. Her dark curls clung
to her damp skin.

The mother smoothed the little girl's forehead and began
weeping.

"She's so hot," the woman sobbed. "She's burning with
fever." She sobbed and sobbed, nestling her face against the

child.

Alfonso wanted to comfort her, but he did not know how. Finally he reached into the pocket of his breeches for the silver amulet his mother had given him on his saint's name day.

He laid it on her lap.

She smiled slightly through her tears, then turned her attention back to the child who was dozing against her breast, the child's tiny hands clutching her mother's hair.

In his sleep he kept seeing the Jews' faces and their haunted eyes. They turned into rats nibbling food. Then he had a dream so vivid that he did not seem to be asleep at all. In it, he was walking down the hallway to his father's study. A glimmer of light shone underneath the door. Something impelled him to push it open.

When he did, he saw that a silver menorah with tall white tapers provided the light. His father and the old man who had tried to abduct him were standing close together, swaying back and forth as they chanted Hebrew prayers. They wore white prayer shawls embroidered with golden threads.

When the old man saw Alfonso, he flapped his arms, and the ends of the shawl became wings. Then he rose slightly off the Persian rug on which he stood, and he floated towards Alfonso. "God be with you, Alfonso," he said in that foreign tongue. But Alfonso understood his words. The old man pushed him outside into the dark hallway and shut the door.

Alfonso would have dismissed it as entirely a dream, but for the golden threads he found upon his pillow when he awakened in the morning.

CHAPTER 2

Emilia was the child and Inés the mother who rode home with Alfonso. Because her fever was so high, the doctor did not expect Emilia to live. In vain had he applied leeches to her to drain the excess blood. His potions had been useless in lowering the fever, and the child had gone into delirium.

Inés lay curled up in a corner of the big canopied bed where her daughter lay. She was weeping not only for her daughter but for her husband, a frail man who had died on the journey and who, like the old Jew's Benji, had been hastily buried in a field. She grieved for her other children, who had all died in infancy.

Doña Luisa Valdez, dressed in black with a fringe of white lace at her throat, bathed the little girl in rose water and gently put a wet cloth between her lips. The child reminded her of her beloved Francesca, over whose grave she had planted a fragrant jasmine.

Emilia began to thrash her arms and legs in delirium. Luisa became greatly perturbed with painful memories of her daughter, who had died at the age of four of lung congestion during a harsh winter. She began saying her rosary in a low, intense voice. A servant gripped the child's feet, while Inés gripped the child's hands to quiet her down.

Don Carlos did not approve of what he termed superstition or folk magic, but Doña Luisa – she whose severe air intimidated the servants – quietly sent for old Diego, the *ensalmador*, or healer, famous in Cádiz for the cures he had effected, which people spoke about in hushed voices.

After dusk the healer came. Candles burned in the dark room. Inés had fallen asleep, overcome with exhaustion.

Emilia, whom Doña Luisa had dressed in a fine white cotton nightgown, lay flushed with color, damp with perspiration, her dark curls spread over the pillow. Although she was almost four, she looked younger, as she was tiny for her age. "A little angel," the *ensalmador* sighed, taken with her. He was short, bulky, dressed in clean but ragged brown tunic and breeches, with heavy sandals. He sighed again and closed his eyes in concentration, then with hands folded in prayer, he muttered words so low that the others could barely hear.

At last he opened his eyes and leaned over the child. He lowered his body so that he was over her, supporting his weight with his hands. Her mouth was parted. He breathed into her mouth, then lowering himself still more, so that he was on top of her, he pressed his lips to hers, and as his breathing adjusted to her rhythm, he blew his own breath into her body and sucked the foul air out of her.

Then he stood up again, laid his hands on her head and muttered an incantation. Doña Luisa pressed silver into his hand, and he vanished.

That night Emilia's fever broke. The household rejoiced, although few knew what had actually happened.

But in the coming days, an undercurrent of tension could be felt in the household. Something was not as it seemed on the surface.

They learned that pirates attacked many ships carrying Jews. Berbers massacred hordes of Jews when they tried to land in Algiers. Through God's blessing, Don Carlos' ships had arrived safely in Constantinople, but many of the passengers died of illness during the journey.

Doña Luisa prayed for hours each day in their private chapel. She said she was praying for her brother, Rodrigo, who had sailed off to the Indies with an explorer named Cristóbal Colón.

CHAPTER 3

A woman's screams rang through the house, awakening a family and servants. Night after night Aunt Silvia's screams would pierce the darkness, giving voice to the fear that permeated the house. Tottering out of her room in her nightgown, she would stumble along the corridor holding a candle dangerously close to her loose hair, her eyes glassy with fright from a nightmare. A maid or Doña Luisa or Inés would comfort her and gently lead her back to bed, placing laurel leaves beneath her pillow, murmuring prayers for protection of her spirit.

A woman so fragile it seemed a breath of air could float her away, Don Carlos' sister Silvia had lived with them ever since her husband died many years ago. Her two sons, Arturo and Diego, worked for Don Carlos, and they, too, had recently departed to oversee offices abroad. Even after news of their safe arrival in Constantinople, Silvia's nightmares continued.

Despite her age, her speaking voice was girlish, but when she sang something altogether different surfaced. Then her voice did not seem to belong to her at all, so pure and strong were the tones that rang through her. Gifted with a fine ear, she could recall the melody and words of a song heard only once. She knew hundreds of songs, both old and new. Not only could she sing the *canto hondo* of Andalusian gypsies, but she knew their dances. Despite her age, her body was supple, and she could move with swift graceful steps.

And she was lonely, for Luisa did not offer her friendship. So when Emilia recovered from her illness, Silvia took the child under her wing, delighted in teaching her songs and dances, and let her strum the strings of her guitar.

Emilia became everyone's child. With her brilliant smile and a face alive with intelligence, she was hard to resist. She loved to mimic people. This earned her applause. Animals were drawn to something intangible about her. Birds in the aviary perched on her shoulder; goats followed at her heels; cats curled in her lap.

Her mother, meanwhile, had become Doña Luisa's personal attendant and attained a closeness to Luisa enjoyed by few others. Doña Luisa came from the north. Fairer-skinned than most Andalusians, she was also of a colder temperament. As a girl she had spent years in a convent, and she had nearly taken nun's vows. Her dignified manner concealed her emotions. However, she warmed to Inés as to a long lost sister. The two women spent long hours together in conversation. Inés brushed her mistress's hair, fetched lavender blossoms to soothe her frequent headaches, drew her baths.

Doña Luisa had taken it upon herself to supervise Inés' religious instruction. She gave Inés a silver and ruby rosary which had been passed down for generations through her mother's family. "Because we are sisters in spirit," she said as she placed it around the other woman's neck and embraced her. She arranged for the family priest, Father Juan, to instruct Inés in the Christian faith. He was a man of extraordinary kindness, and he helped to allay the bitterness Inés may have felt as an *anusa*, or forced Christian. In the privacy of confession, little by little he drew her out, for she sensed that she could trust him.

As for Alfonso, he looked forward to Father Juan's daily visits. Father Juan taught him his *abecaría*, the lessons given to small children. The priest's love was like warm spring sunshine. Alfonso would curl up on his lap and beg, "Tell me stories." And the priest told tales of saints and miracles, the Virgin and Our Lord, and the Apostles.

Under Father Juan's influence, the child poured his soul into religion. Each night he prayed at an altar of cedarwood at the foot of his bed. Each morning he joined his family in their chapel. The soft golden morning light that poured in through the window seemed to gleam brighter as he prayed with all his heart, pouring out his desire for God.

When he grew older, he also prayed in the Cathedral. The smell of frankincense, the lighted wax tapers, vaulted ceilings, and the stained glass windows in beautiful designs of scarlet, purple, green, and gold assailed his senses in such a way that he felt transported beyond himself.

"*Benedicat vos Deus omnipotens. . . .*" the officiating priest's chanting voice strengthened the spell. In the semi-darkness shadows flickered. He watched a swallow fly from an eave towards a dark corner. As he took the communion wafer into his mouth, he seemed to feel Christ's presence, as if He had entered Alfonso's very soul, and Alfonso seemed to float out of himself, his body dissolving into the vaulted space all around him.

Sometimes when he prayed very intensely, or when he fasted, he had visions, and he also felt Christ's presence.

When he told Father Juan of these visions, the priest grew concerned. "Be careful, my child," he warned. "Sometimes the Devil insinuates himself into the shape of an angel or even Our Lord. Don't speak of these visions to anyone. I will pray for the protection of your soul."

Alfonso was a precocious child, intensely sensitive to the unspoken thoughts and emotions of others. At times his brother Miguel tormented him cruelly. Then Alfonso's anger would rise to a fever pitch, and he would lash out at his older brother with fists, feet, even his teeth. He hated his older brother Miguel with a fierce black hatred that he prayed God to expunge from his heart and forgive. Once his brother had locked him in a chamber underground, and Alfonso had screamed at the top of his lungs, until finally Miguel, gloating with power, had released him.

Eight times a day a *muezzin's* horn sounded from the mosque. Situated near the former Jewish ghetto, somehow the shabby old mosque had escaped closure, despite the formal ban on worship of Mohammed which had long been in effect. Each time it sounded, the old blind Arab tutor Ishan would interrupt whatever he was doing and drop to his knees in prayer.

He had lived with the family for many years. When Alfonso was three, Ishan had taken him on his lap beneath the hot sun in the courtyard and had taught the child how to trace numbers and letters in a sand-filled tray, just as he had taught Alfonso's brothers years earlier. He had taught them to read and write in both Arabic and Spanish before they advanced to other tutors.

By the time Emilia and Inés joined the family Alfonso had nearly outgrown Ishan. Emilia, curious and eager to explore everything, clamored to join Alfonso in his lessons. Old Ishan had little to do, and he was glad to teach her. However, this presented a delicate situation, as Emilia and her mother occupied a position halfway between servants and family members. None of the servant's children had received tutoring. For that matter, Inés herself could only make out Hebrew letters. At first Don Carlos was reluctant to let Ishan teach the little girl.

But she had insisted. "*Please* let me learn," Emilia pleaded with Don Carlos, and the intensity in her large dark eyes moved him. So she and Alfonso began to study together. A close bond developed between them, despite the difference in their ages.

Then on the eve of a cardinal's visit, officials boarded shut the doors of the old mosque, and the muezzin's horn stopped sounding. In the time that followed, Ishan, completely undone, would weep unashamedly.

He died a few months later.

CHAPTER 4

All through the land the Church was tightening its grip. Father Juan's superior, Bishop Bernardo, a tall, gaunt man with cold eyes, demanded confession at his private quarters from Alfonso, who was then nine years old. He asked the child troubling questions. Did Alfonso's parents cross themselves when they spoke the names of the Holy Trinity? How frequently did they bathe? Did they light candles on Friday nights and put on clean apparel? Alfonso murmured that he did not know.

When he relayed these questions to Father Juan, a shadow passed over Juan's rough-hewn face. But he quickly composed himself, saying that the Bishop wanted to be sure that children under his wing were growing up in truly Christian homes. "Lighting candles on Fridays is a custom followed by Jews. As for bathing, it expresses attachment to the body, which can lead to mortal sin. The spirit alone is eternal, my son. Your parents are exemplary in their faith." Juan's voice trembled.

Despite the priest's reassurance, that night Alfonso lay sleepless with fear. He hoped he had not said anything that would injure his parents in the Bishop's eyes.

Fear and suspicion were everywhere.

The Office of the Holy Inquisition established a council in Cádiz. Its task was to ferret out heretics, particularly those who practiced Judaism in secret. They employed *familiares* as undercover spies. Faltering over the words of the Pater Noster or the Ave Maria in church, neglecting to cross oneself when speaking the names of Our Saviour or the Blessed Virgin, not attending mass regularly, refusing to eat pork, all these details

could assume ominous significance. Conversos were particularly suspect, although people said that Torquemada himself
was one. Those who still secretly practiced Judaism were
called *Marranos*, which is to say, "pigs".

"Are we New Christians?" Alfonso asked his father.

Don Carlos' lips quivered with indignation. "Both your
mother and I trace our Christian lineage back to the Goths."
He showed his son the fragile parchment scrolls, enclosed in a
velvet-lined box, which contained their family trees over centuries. He let Alfonso peruse the scrolls, lingering over the
names. "Your mother's family, the Echevarías and Castillos,
came from the mountainous province of Burgos. Mine came
from Toledo. See here . . . over two hundred years ago Alfonso
López was a warrior for Pedro the Cruel. He captured cities
for the Church. We named you after him."

So Alfonso should have been assured. But still the fear in
the air crept into his nerves. One night his Aunt Silvia was
awakened by a particularly vivid nightmare. As usual, her
screams woke nearly everyone. Crying out with fear, she stag-
gered through the hallways. "Flames are burning me!" she
screamed. Inés took the lighted candle from her shaky fingers.

"Oh, Silvia," said Doña Luisa, with a glance of complicity at Inés, as if to say what a fool that woman is. But tender-
hearted Inés, flickering her lashes in response, gazed at Silvia
with sympathy, put her arm around the half-conscious
woman, and gently led her back to her room.

Doña Luisa realized that she herself was trembling.

The next day they learned that Count Sergio Mendez de
Monteros, along with his wife and two daughters, had been
arrested by the Inquisition. The web of fear in Alfonso's
household tightened. Doña Luisa could scarcely breathe, for
the Count and his family were their friends. Don Carlos paced
back and forth in their bed chamber. Usually so disciplined in
his display of emotions, he now revealed his agitation. Neither
dared voice their thoughts, for who knew what servants might
be listening.

Several days later, when they learned that the Count's family had managed to escape from prison, leaving behind all their possessions, Carlos and Luisa embraced with relief. Luisa sobbed against her husband's shoulder.

The family grew more faithful in their attendance at mass. Carlos and Luisa donated one thousand maravedis for construction of a new chapel inside the Cathedral.

Like molten wax, Alfonso's fear transmuted into a passion for the Divine. He continued to pray at the little altar by his bed. Sometimes he would smell a fragrance that had no discernible source. Sometimes the room glowed brighter, and he felt the presence of spirits.

He had begun to study philosophy and natural science, among other subjects, with a tutor from Avignon named Gaillard. At times this new knowledge raised troubling questions. Then he would go to Father Juan, who usually managed to reconcile his intellectual conflicts with Church doctrines and to soothe him.

When he was twelve, there was a drought. Crops failed for lack of water. Children died for lack of proper nourishment. There were outbreaks of plague. Rage surged through the townsfolk.

That August the Holy Office decreed an *auto da fé*.

Before the first crowing of cocks, while the sky was still dark and glimmering with stars, drums began to beat in a low, monotonous, yet unsettling rhythm. They could be heard throughout the city. The drums beat rolled on for hours, an ominous undertow of sound.

The Mendez house now served as a prison. At dawn, prisoners were taken from their quarters. Barefoot and chained to one another, they limped to the Cathedral to receive Bishop Bernardo's blessing before proceeding on to the Plaza, where they would be sentenced. They wore coarse yellow *sambenito* robes of penitence, as well as ridiculous tall cone hats. Many could barely walk. Some traveled in carts pulled by mules or donkeys, because their bodies had been so broken by torture.

The prisoners were surrounded by mobs who jeered and threw stones as well as the contents of slop pails. They had to be forcibly restrained by guards from attacking and tearing the prisoners to pieces.

In the main plaza, a raised platform had been constructed for Inquisition judges and religious dignitaries. Surrounding it were stands for spectators. By the time church bells rang Terce, commoners already crammed the benches in their section and were standing up. Aristocratic families sat in special boxes shaded by awnings of purple damask embroidered with golden crosses and filigrees. Some families had traveled many leagues from the countryside, where they owned large estates. Their peasants crowded into the commoners' sections.

To the side was a section of shaded seats reserved for monks and nuns, among them Father Juan.

Trumpets sounded as dignitaries, all in black Dominican robes, arrived on fine chestnut horses. First came the Cardinal, wielding a banner with a green cross on a white field. Then came the Archbishop. He carried a blue banner emblazoned with the white cross of Our Lord.

Finally, as drums rolled, the Inquisitor General rode in astride a white stallion.

"By honor invested in my office, I swear to defend the Holy Faith. May Mercy and Justice prevail, and may God shed His grace on those about to receive punishment," declared the Inquisitor through a bull's horn, which magnified the sound of his voice.

The dignitaries dismounted and took their seats on a raised dais, shaded by a splendid awning of white and gold.

Beneath the platform, in the direct glare of the sun, huddled the prisoners, fifteen in number.

"Look, there's the *ensalmador*," whispered Emilia to her mother. Many times she had heard the tale of how the old healer saved her life. She clutched her mother's sleeve, but Inés stared straight ahead, choking back her emotions. The old man huddled in a cart, unable even to sit up. He had been tortured. His feet were swathed in ragged bandages. His face was unnaturally pale, his eyes glazed.

The sun rose higher. It grew hot and sticky. The light of the sun became a merciless glare. And the drums were still beating from afar. Their insistent rhythm increased Alfonso's anxiety. His father, Don Carlos, gave no hint of emotion while he watched the proceedings. Nor did his mother. She and Don Carlos sat together, their shoulders lightly touching. But Miguel, the cruel, mischievous one, turned to look at Alfonso with expression of disgust. "Bastards," he muttered into Alfonso's ear.

During a recess, a juggler threw brightly colored balls into the air. Two dwarfs performed their antics. One disrobed to the waist, displaying a sickly, malformed body, while the other scourged him with a slender twig.

The smells of roast pork, grilled onions and fish filled the air.

People hawked amulets and holy relics.

Women sold pastries from large wooden trays.

Small boys and girls sold fried anchovies on sticks.

Alfonso wished that Rafael were here to put a comforting arm around his shoulder and murmur some phrase, perhaps in Latin, which would make sense of it all. But his oldest brother had sailed to the distant Orient.

Somewhat apart from the family sat his tutor, Gaillard. Squat and muscular, with a mop of wild black hair, Gaillard was hunched over in a maroon doublet. Alfonso sensed Gaillard's inward skepticism about the Church, and he wondered what the tutor would make of all this.

By midday, sweat drenched Alfonso's breeches, shirt, and hatband. Servants brought them a light meal of fruit and bread in hampers along with sweet almond water, and afterwards there was a recess, during which people filed out and stretched their cramped bodies. The Duchess of Cádiz, who had been sitting in a special place of honor, waved to his moth-

er. As young girls, they had befriended each other at their convent. Doña Luisa and Inés joined the Duchess. The three
women talked quietly.

After the noon recess, judges continued to question the
prisoners. They passed judgment on lesser crimes such as
thieving, bigamy, and sorcery. The prisoners were condemned
to floggings and imprisonment, with varying degrees of harshness.

The hours wore on.

It was the hottest day of the year.

The crowd's rage increased to a fever pitch.

Now the judges were trying those who had been accused
of Judaizing. Two men carried the *ensalmador* to the platform. He struggled to sit up, but could not, as his spine had
been injured. Finally, they placed a cushion behind him.

"Dost thou believe that God is One in essence and Three
in person." "Yes, my father, I believe," "Then why did you
consult Hebrew rabbinical texts?" "Holy father, I erred, and I
beg forgiveness. . . . "

In the end, despite his entreaties, the old *ensalmador* was
given over into the hands of the State.

The State sentenced him to burn at the stake.

Seven other Judaizers were also given over into the hands
of the State and they, too, were condemned to burn. For the
Church, no matter how it tortured people, would take no
human life. As for the Mendez family who had been fortunate
enough to flee, all of them were sentenced to burn in effigy.

Then the Archbishop in his black robes stood up, a lone
figure against the scorched earth and white-hot sky. He railed
against the secret Judaizers. "Christians and Jews alike
despise them!" he cried through the bull horn.

"They corrupt Spain and the Church from within. These
people have only pretended to be Christians. They have
robbed you of your jobs and your spiritual strength. They give
advice at Court. They have married into noble families. They
take Christ's name in vain. Nothing can change their corrupt

natures. They scoff at you all, even those who are here now. We will find you out!"

A roar went through the crowd.

His robes swung as he turned around, and his eyes swept the crowd, lingering over certain noble families. His fingers clawed the air, and his eyes glittered. It was said that he was extreme in his penances, that he slept in a hair shirt, lashed himself with cords, and underwent prolonged fasts.

"Unhappy fragments of the Synagogue! Miserable relics of Judaism!" the Archbishop cried. Again, his glance alighted on noble families. "You are objects of contempt even to Jews! Yes, even the Jews despise you, for you are so ignorant that you cannot even observe the laws of the Jews. So perverted are your natures that you no longer live either as Jews or Catholics. Let God's will be done. Let flames consume all heretics and purify the soul of Spain."

The crowd roared louder.

Doña Luisa's breath froze.

At dusk, as the red orb of the sun sank beneath the horizon, the closing ceremonies took place. Monks chanted an Exorcism, and a choir sang psalms in pure, precise harmonies.

When they left, Emilia walked alone. Overtaking her, Alfonso discovered that she was crying. In her black brocade dress with its white lace collar, her graceful slippers, and her hair carefully curled by Aunt Silvia, she looked like a little infanta. But the tears made muddy streaks along her cheeks, when she wiped them with her hands.

"What happened?" he asked.

She only sobbed harder.

"Tell me."

"No."

She ran towards Aunt Silvia, who was tottering along exhausted by the day's events. Sobbing, Emilia flung her arms around her. "I love you. I will always love you," she sobbed.

That night pitch-filled torches lit the streets as the eight condemned prisoners were brought to the *brasero*, the stakes near the northern gate of the city.

They were tied to stakes above piles of straw.

"If you repent and accept Our Lord, I will strangle you now and spare you further pain," said the Inquisitor to the *ensalmador*.

"Vile demon," hissed the old man. "I have suffered beyond wanting to save this poor, broken body. May you and your descendants be cursed for all time. I curse the Church. I curse the false Messiah. I curse you all!"

Flames licked his feet. "Shema Israel Adonai Elohenu, Adonai Ehad," he chanted. Other prisoners joined in, until smoke suffocated their voices.

Far off, people sang and danced in the streets. The flames of the *auto da fé* intensified passions of those who lay together that night.

CHAPTER 5

Emilia knelt in the Cathedral and prayed: *My friends, Teresa and Manuela, laughed at Aunt Silvia and called her a witch. That scares me, because I don't want the Inquisitors to flog her, as they did the tailor's widow. They stripped her naked down to her waist. Her breasts drooped like a cow's teats for all to see. How shameful it was. They whipped her until she was bloody and screaming with pain. The priest performed an exorcism, and they sent her to prison. But she was no witch. She was just a kind old woman, a little strange in her ways like Aunt Silvia. She used to give me almond pastries.*

I'm scared for Aunt Silvia. She is so tender and merry with me. With her love she has planted her gifts of song and dance inside me, where they bloom like flowers. God forgive me, but I love Aunt Silvia even a little bit more than Mamá, who left her family and became Christian to save my life. Maybe they will say she is a heretic. and arrest her, too.

I will watch very carefully. I am sharp-eyed. I will find out if any of our servants are familiares. Elena, the chambermaid may be spying on us. I don't like the way she looks at Mamá. I will warn Aunt Silvia and Mamá. Maybe all three of us should run away . We can disguise ourselves in men's clothing and sail to Italy.

Should I tell Alfonso? He still helps me with my lessons, now we're studying with Gaillard. But I'm only allowed to be with them in the morning, and he helps me keep up. Sometimes I think Alfonso sees into my mind when he says exactly the words I'm thinking.

Holy Mother of God, protect us. I will say 100 Ave Marias
and 50 Paternosters every single day on my rosary. Oh please
God have mercy on Aunt Silvia and Mamá, and all of us.

Emilia straightened up from the bench on which she had
been kneeling. She bowed and made the sign of the cross
before the Virgin's statue. The cool darkness of the Cathedral,
with its odors of incense and cool plaster soothed her. The
soaring heights of the pillars and domed ceiling seemed to let
her mind roam free in the expansive space.

She decided to tell Alfonso what had happened.

"Aunt Silvia's no witch," he said angrily, when he heard
how the other girls taunted her about Silvia's being a sorcer-
ess. "These are just little girls' make-believe stories. No one
would believe them."

However, he himself was perturbed.

The Inquisition permeated all their lives. Even the bril-
liance of the midday sun took on an ominous quality.

"Christ teaches love, but the Inquisitors are full of
hatred. Why?" Alfonso asked Father Juan. The priest could
offer no answers, except to murmur, "Our Savior is merciful,
my son. Cling to Jesus Christ. Cling to Jesus Christ alone."

"But they are wicked."

"Even these walls may have ears," said the priest in a low
voice. "Beware of careless words."

They were wandering through the *aljama*, the former
Jewish quarter. The cobblestones echoed beneath them. Few
people had ventured to move into the vacant houses, and an
eerie stillness pervaded. In the shade of a doorway, a mongrel
dozed. Shadowy cats chased their prey among the white-
washed buildings.

People told tales of blood libel. At a wayside inn,
pranksters had opened a traveler's knapsack to find crumbled
bits of *matzah*. They claimed that the knapsack also contained
a child's bloodstained garments, and that Jews had sacrificed
a child.

Familiares continued their spying. Neighbors, friends, servants, even family members had been known to betray each other. They might be motivated by religious zeal, desire for revenge, fear of punishment, or desire for gain. It was said that, in their eagerness to please the Holy Inquisitors, informers even made up incriminating evidence.

Bishop Bernardo spoke of the significance of *limpieza de sangre*, or purity of blood. It was fortunate indeed that Don Carlos' family were Old Christians. However, that did not exempt them from scrutiny.

On the day Alfonso first experienced this, he was in the barber's shop getting his hair cut.

The barber, a plump man with beady eyes, wore the emblem of a *regidor*, one of the elite members of the local Council of the Inquisition. He wore the Inquisition's emblem – a gleaming silver cross with an olive branch and dagger.

As his knife cut close to Alfonso's ear, he whispered to the boy, "I hear the Marranos hold secret ceremonies for their sons when they approach manhood."

"Do they?" said Alfonso, uneasy that the barber had brought up this subject.

"You'll soon be a man," said the barber. He cleared his throat. "They say your father has befriended Jews. He took in the Jewess Inés and her child."

"The other Jews would have killed her when she accepted Our Lord."

Sunlight sparkled on the silver cross on the barber's leather vest. As the barber cut again, his knife grazed Alfonso's cheek, drawing a drop of blood, but Alfonso did not flinch. He displayed a calmness worthy of his father.

As if drawn to the dark turbulence of the City, lepers took up their abode just outside the Eastern Gate. Whenever travelers passed through, a crowd of these wretched creatures would approach them, clamoring for alms.

Penitents in *sambenito* robes became a common sight.

They stumbled through the streets, while monks goaded them with whips and crowds jeered and shouted insults. Even young children were not spared. Little boys and girls as young as five or six were forced to don robes, sharing the family shame. People took savage delight in throwing waste from their chamberpots upon the tiny bodies, whose faces would be streaked with excrement and tears.

Autumn winds blew. Winter rains began to fall. It grew colder, and the days grew shorter.

Alfonso and Miguel would sometimes ride to the beach with Gaillard, to practice swordsmanship. Beneath wintry clouds, while gray-green waves rolled against their horse's forefeet, they would gallop along and practice parrying and thrusting at each other, usually with wooden sticks in place of swords.

Gaillard also tutored them as well as Emilia (who had clamored to continue her studies after Ishan died) in mathematics, Greek, Latin, and modern languages, as well as science and philosophy.

He was truly a man of many talents. Of medium height, with wiry black hair and an acrobat's body, he possessed a certain recklessness.

"Ah, the Inquisition," he said one afternoon, as they were discussing the Roman Stoics. Then in French, he added, "The black dragon! How frightened people are. As Epicetus says, human nature doesn't change. The Romans threw Christians into pits with wild beasts. And now it's the Christian's turn for revenge." He gave a wry little smile.

He was the only one who dared speak this way.

"Why did you leave Avignon?" Miguel asked suspiciously.

"I am a wanderer, an eternal wanderer," said Gaillard, still speaking in French.

He was not insensible to women's charms, and many evenings found him sleeping in the soft arms of women who lived in ramshackle buildings beside the harbor.

Whenever Emilia appeared, the tutor's eyes would light

up. "*La belle jeune fille*," he would call her, sweeping off his hat as he bowed before her. She loved his playfulness. He would stand close and tell her jokes in a low voice that made her laugh. Her mother and Silvia both grew somewhat alarmed at his attentions to the young girl. "Don't encourage him," warned Inés.

CHAPTER 6

Amsterdam, October, 1498

Glistening, ever-shifting waves at sea. Sunlight gave way to heavy storm clouds as the ship Alfonso and his father were on traveled north. Cold rain poured down. Wind pierced their faces and bodies. Then huge waves began to sweep over the decks.

All who could took cover below.

The ship pitched violently, and Alfonso vomited into a slop jar. Alone in their tiny cabin, he wondered where his father had gone. He tried to keep his balance as the flooring rocked beneath him while he made his way along the dark narrow corridor to the dining salon, where most of the passengers had already gathered. As this was a cargo ship, there were only a handful, all of them shaky and frightened. Don Carlos was not among them.

They were praying aloud.

Alfonso prayed silently that his father was safe. Hours later he found his father sprawled out on the bottom bunk. But Don Carlos only mumbled something incomprehensible when Alfonso asked where he had been.

By the grace of God, they emerged safely into calmer waters. Several days later they reached the Port of Amsterdam on the gray Zuider Zee. Late in the afternoon they dropped anchor.

In the Customs House, Alfonso sipped warm ale. It was a strange bitter taste, but to his liking. His father was talking with officials, who were all dressed in black. He had not realized that his father spoke Dutch. The sounds were like the German he had studied. He saw his father unobtrusively press gold *maravedis* into their hands.

Smoke from the stove was making him cough, and so he went outside for fresh air. Letting his eyes wander over the unfamiliar landscape – leaden sky and water, flat horizon interrupted with red brick buildings and bare trees – he idly watched the last of the sailors leave their ship, which rocked gently at anchor. Then he could scarcely believe his eyes when, in the growing darkness, he saw faint outlines of ghostly bodies, about a dozen in all, descend the gangplank. They breathed out wisps of clouds into the cold air.

As he moved closer to the ship, he saw that they wore bulky clothing. The women were wrapped in heavy shawls. Up close, he discerned familiar faces – a fishmonger with his wife and child, a cloth weaver, a scrivener. They embraced families and friends who emerged out of the darkness to welcome them.

He was unaware that his father had joined him until he felt Don Carlos' warm hand on his shoulder and looked up into his face, half obscured by his thick beard.

The scrivener had detached himself from the group. He strode in a purposeful way towards Don Carlos, fell to his knees, and kissed Don Carlos' hand. Then he said something in Hebrew, to which Don Carlos responded in the same tongue, bidding him rise. To Alfonso's ears, the Hebrew sounds resonated of harsh desert winds.

The scrivener was weeping.

A black mass of tangled emotions arose in Alfonso, as what he had long sensed but tried to hide from himself became apparent.

He recalled his childhood vision of the Old Jew and his father praying together in Hebrew. He recalled the mysterious golden threads on his pillow. Had an angel left them there? He thought of the fear that ran rampant beneath the surface in his household and of his Aunt Silvia's nightmares.

"Come, the boatman's waiting," said his father.

They were going to Rafael's house. Alfonso had not seen his beloved brother for several years, and he had been filled with excitement at the prospect of being with him again. But now suspicions swarmed through his mind. Why had Rafael been away for so long?

"Those stowaways are Jews," said Alfonso.

"*Claro*," said his father. "In Amsterdam, may it please God, my passengers will be safe. Here they can openly worship in the way of their ancestors."

A raw wind was blowing. The moon had just begun to rise, a faint yellow sliver against the horizon's edge. Alfonso shivered. The wind blew through his cloak, chilling him to the bone.

"You risked your life and all our lives to smuggle them out," Alfonso said.

After a pause, Don Carlos responded. "What does a man have if not his honor and his conscience? In the end, it's God, not man who judges."

They walked on. Alfonso's boots felt heavy with each step he took along the muddy road.

"Did the crewmen know?"

"Only a few."

"Then we're at their mercy."

"Our fates are always in God's hands," said his father.

Their boots were the same dark leather, covered with mud. They walked with strides of the same length.

"Father, what about us? Are we Jews?" The words in his throat stuck like the claws of birds.

Don Carlos stood very still. For a long time he said nothing. At last he spoke, his voice low in the darkness. "Yes," he said.

"Then we are Marranos – swine – that's what they call Jews who pretend to be Christians! You've hidden this from me. You've all lied to me and deceived me."

"We were *anusim* – which means that we were forced to convert," said his father said, grasping Alfonso's wrists and looking hard into Alfonso's eyes. His own gleamed in the moonlight. "They baptised your ancestors at sword's point. A mob killed your mother's parents because they refused. She grew up an orphan."

Alfonso struggled free from Don Carlos' grip.

"What about our ancestral tree? It shows pure Christian blood." Alfonso thought of the yellowed parchments with their faded ink in leather bindings.

"Anything can be bought for a price. As for our coat of arms, a clever artist designed it. Your grandfather – my father – a gifted storyteller, spread tales of our illustrious history."

They reached a canal where a boatman awaited them. Their three leather trunks had already been loaded onto the flat-bottomed rowboat, and now they, too, climbed in.

As the boatman heaved with effort, the oars cut the water with a steady, plopping sound. Other boats and barges with lanterns attached to their bowsprits also moved along the canal, which was like a narrow river.

"Gold buys silence, as perhaps you observed a little while ago. But in the end, our lives are in the hands of the Lord. It is how we live that counts," Don Carlos said.

They glided beneath bridges.

It began raining. They were only partially covered by the awning, and cold rain beat against their faces.

Alfonso gripped the rosary inside the pocket of his cloak. In shock, he murmured his beads.

We are Jews. Marranos. *Pigs. The servants say we have tails hidden beneath our trousers and that we menstruate like women*

Jesus help me.

They glided on in the darkness, cold and wet from the rain which kept on falling.

"New Christians can be our cruelest persecutors." Don Carlos' voice cut into Alfonso's thoughts. "It was Torquemada who persuaded Queen Isabella to expel the Jews. He has burned thousands of *Judaisers* at the stake, and he would gladly burn the lot of us."

The oars sounded against the water. Alfonso gazed at the

boatman's straining back. He was a thin man, covered with a brown cloak and knit cap. Did the boatman understand Castilian? If so, would he betray them?

"Why did our family remain Jews?" Alfonso asked.

"Our ancestors valued their Jewish faith even more than their lives. *This is who we are*," said his father. It's in our bones and in our blood. If we lose our heritage, we are truly lost souls. Its teaching – of which you are regrettably ignorant – contain treasure beyond price."

"You have all deceived me."

Alfonso had half an urge to throw himself into the icy water. As he could not swim, he would sink to the bottom like a stone. Then he would no longer feel this unbearable pain.

His father put his arms around him. "Alfonso." Don Carlos' voice broke with emotion. "I wish we hadn't been forced to hide who we were. We all know families who have burned at the stake because of the idle chatter of five-year-olds."

"You hid the truth all these years. I sensed it. But I did not want to believe it!"

Don Carlos rubbed the boy's shoulders. His own heart ached. There was ever-present danger. What if a sailor, unbeknownst to him, held a grudge or were held for questioning by Inquisitors? What then? A few words could undo them all. Why then did he persist in smuggling out Jews? Someone must shoulder the burden, and if not he, then who else?

"Our heritage is a treasure beyond price." he repeated. "When you learn more about it, I pray that you will realize this."

Codfish squirmed in a thick net which fishermen were hoisting out of the water onto a dock lit with many lanterns. Alfonso gazed at the fish. He felt like one of those poor struggling creatures.

His father continued. "You have seen the wicked deeds performed in the name of Christianity. Satan attacks the Jews through the Church. Alfonso, think of what the Inquisition

has done. Think of the tortures it inflicts in the name of God,
Christ, and the Holy Ghost. What a ridiculous concept – the
Trinity. There is only one God. Jesus was no more than a
prophet. According to Jewish belief, the Messiah has not yet
appeared on earth."

A chill ran through Alfonso. In his father's impassioned
expression he perceived something demonic.

"Father Juan, your favorite priest, is one of us. He's a
cousin of your mother's, and related to you by blood."

"Stop!" Alfonso cried. "Say no more! You've all been living a lie. Bishop Bernardo was right. Lies have corrupted all
of you, and you've corrupted me. I too could turn informer. I
understand Torquemada."

The lantern attached to the bow lit his father's features.
His father did not move a muscle. He seemed paralyzed. Then
at last he spoke. "I would never have told you if I hadn't trusted you."

"Does Miguel know?"

His father shook his head. "No," he whispered, and he
sighed. "His nature is too volatile. When he drinks too much,
he talks too freely, and he picks quarrels. We've placed our
trust in Rafael and in you."

The boat continued on, and Alfonso, overcome, listened
to the sound of the oars against the water. So Father Juan,
whom he had loved and in whom he had confided so freely, all
this time had been looking upon Alfonso's innocent Christian
faith with cynicism. Ah, now Alfonso understood the fury of
Christians who, like him, had been duped and betrayed. He
had no one now. He was truly alone, except for a distant God.
He wished they could go on until they dropped off the edge of
an earth as flat as ancients believed it to be. Then sea monsters
would devour him. Then he would no longer need to think or
decide or act.

At last they anchored at an empty, rotting pier lit by a
small lantern that swayed back and forth from a rope. The
boatman helped them carry their trunks to Rafael's door, and

a servant showed them into a warm, smoky room.

Rafael greeted them with joy. His cheeks were flushed, and he had gained weight. In the Jewish manner he had grown long earlocks, and he wore a tight-fitting cap of black felt, while the rest of his costume – heavy woolen shirt, waistcoat, breeches, wooden clogs – was in the style of a Dutch burgher. "Welcome!" he cried, embracing Alfonso and holding him tightly. "Don't be frightened," he added, taking off his cap. Beneath it his black hair squashed down flat against his skull. "I'm not the devil. Perhaps father has explained to you."

"Yes, he did." said Alfonso.

"This is my home now," said Rafael. "I will never return to Spain."

The crucifix that hung around Alfonso's neck seemed to burn into his chest.

"Ah, but you and Papá are both cold and wet. We must warm you."

Alfonso and his father put on dry clothing. A serving maid who looked no older than a child served them herring and schnapps, which warmed the throat and belly.

While Don Carlos and Rafael conferred, Alfonso rested on the floor by the fire, overwhelmed by what had been revealed to him and by Rafael's transformation.

"This is all very painful for him," said Don Carlos.

"For me, it wasn't so difficult," said Rafael. "I've always been more skeptical by nature. Furthermore, when I learned of our past the Inquisition hadn't yet become a monstrous organization."

After Alfonso woke up, Rafael introduced him to his wife, Hannah, a fair-skinned blue-eyed woman from German lands. By force of habit, Alfonso bowed deeply. Hannah laughed with delight and said something to Rafael in Dutch. Then she pulled Alfonso over to the blue and white tiled stove in the center of the room, and she showed him their baby daughter who lay sleeping in a cradle. Sarah was only six weeks old. Tiny, plump, serene in her sleep, fair wisps of hair stuck out beneath her crocheted bonnet. Her skin was olive, like Rafael's.

The house was small, gloomy, and cramped, very different from the spacious family home in Cádiz. It had red tile floors and white-washed walls which were dingy from the smoke of oil lamps. Hannah and Rafael conferred with each other, again in Dutch, which was apparently their common language. Alfonso could make out only names of family members, including his own, which Hannah repeated several times in thick, guttural tones.

Hannah lifted the infant from the cradle, and as she did her face filled with soft joy. Sarah gave a cry but did not awaken. Sitting down in a dark corner, Hannah swathed them both in her large shawl and undid the top of her bodice in order to nurse the baby.

The little maid served them dinner, which consisted of cabbage stew, codfish, and moist wheatcakes, along with more of the heavy brown ale Alfonso had first tasted a few hours earlier.

He had no appetite, and the ale turned his stomach.

After dinner Hannah rocked the baby to sleep in her cradle, while the men retired to Rafael's study. Rafael's study was crowded with furniture, and his bookcase was overflowing with books. Alfonso stared at the Hebrew lettering on leather spines.

They told him that Amsterdam was only a temporary haven, as all cities had been since the fall of the Temple in ancient Jerusalem. Any day, people might rise up against them. Rafael was prepared to flee with his little family, should Philip the Fair decide to impose Spanish laws upon them.

Who could foretell the future? The Jews always had to leave the lands in which they had settled.

"Until we regain the Holy Land," said Don Carlos.

They told him that by the grace of God, King Philip had not set foot in his northern provinces for many years. Furthermore, the Flemish burghers were by nature more tolerant than Spaniards.

"Perhaps it's the land, or perhaps the climate," said Rafael. "The land here is so flat. Perhaps the absence of the burning heat of our summers, the absence of steep mountains and deep valleys, endows them with temperaments that are less fiery."

However, they were prepared to flee at any moment, should the situation change suddenly for the worse, as had happened time and again for hundreds of years.

"Commoners hate us for our talents. They say we deprive them of their wealth, when in truth without us they would fare badly."

"Maimonides wrote that it was better to convert than to die," said Rafael. "if we have outwardly professed false beliefs, it's so that our children may survive. When God made his covenant with Abraham, He chose us as His people."

"Each of us is tested," added his father.

Alfonso sat in silence, absorbing their words. He leaned back in his chair, tilting it so that he nearly fell. Then with a jerk, he righted it.

"The Church has perverted Jesus' teachings," added Don Carlos, his voice rising with emotion. "It has made scapegoats of the Jews in order to enrich its own treasuries and has united the common people with an enemy on which they can blame their miseries, their plagues, and their famines."

"The oldest son in a family of *anusim* often becomes a priest. I would have taken Orders if I hadn't married Hannah," said Rafael.

"Why do you compound your hypocrisy?" asked Alfonso.

"Only priests can study Hebrew without arousing suspicion," said his father.

"So that's why Juan became a priest."

"Yes. He was the oldest."

"Did Mother's family really come from the north of Spain?"

"Ah, I wish it were so, for people are more tolerant

there!" said Don Carlos. "If they had lived in the north, they might still be alive. Actually they lived in Madrid, and they were killed by a mob led by Dominican monks. Your mother and her brothers were saved by a neighbor woman who hid them away until the mob's fury had died down. Later on, her cousin Juan's family sent her to a convent."

"So she, too, only pretended."

"How could she believe in a Christ in whose name her parents had been murdered?"

There were many questions Alfonso wanted to ask. He wondered if his father and brother had believed in Christ as Savior when they were children. But it was too painful just now to ask any of the questions that circled, half formed, through his mind.

"You say that the oldest son generally becomes a priest, but Rafael has married. Do you want me to be ordained?" asked Alfonso, staring at the flickering flame of an oil lamp on the table.

Rafael and Don Carlos exchanged glances.

"Certainly you rather than Miguel," said Don Carlos.

"Miguel will bring about our ruin," muttered Alfonso, scarcely aware of what he was saying.

"May God protect us!" said Rafael.

Suddenly, unable to bear it any longer, Alfonso seized a Hebrew book and hurled it to the floor. Its pages spread out on the dark tile floor; its binding broken.

"This is writing of the Devil!" cried Alfonso.

His father and brother looked at him with pale, shocked faces. But underneath their grave looks, Alfonso perceived the Devil's mocking smile.

He strode out of the room. Hastily he put on his cloak and boots.

"Take care!" cried his father, as Alfonso left the house.

"It was nearly midnight, and the moon shone dimly through heavy clouds. Barely conscious of where he was going, he followed a muddy path above the canal.

Running. Walking. Walking. The mud grew softer. With each step he was sinking a little more. Evidently he had strayed off the road. Now the mud came up to his ankles. He must have wandered into a marsh of what they called "devil's sand". Sheep and men alike sank into it, never to emerge. A huge marsh like this lay west of Cádiz, and the unfortunate creatures who stumbled into it were absorbed in its depths.

So this is how he was to die.

Thy will be done, he thought in despair, cold and wet but feverish with emotion. *Give me a sign if You want me to live. Give me a sign. Christian or Jew or dead? A sign. Right hand Christian. Left hand Jew. Left Jew. Right Christian.* By now the mud reached his calves.

A branch whipped him across the face. He reached out for it, feeling its strength. A shaft of moonlight suddenly burned through the clouds. He pulled himself up, clinging to the branch with all his strength, and at last managed to hoist himself up against the crotch of the tree. He realized he had pulled himself to the left. This was the sign.

Thy will be done.

He huddled against the tree until it began to grow light and he could discern a path of stones that led back to the road. After a while he came upon a small brick church, but its door was locked. This, too, he took as a sign. He felt for the polished beads of the rosary inside his breeches pocket, pulled it out, and gave it a farewell kiss.

At last, after some difficulty, he found his way back to the house, cold, muddy, hungry, and tired beyond all measure. When he entered, his father gave a cry and gripped him tightly in his arms. His beard brushed Alfonso's cheek, and his eyes were wet with tears.

At first Alfonso's throat and tongue felt paralyzed. Finally he spoke. "I will do what you wish."

For the next three days Alfonso was confined to his bed with fever. Nightmare visions tormented him in his restless

sleep. Then one cold frosty morning he awakened, still feverish, but too restless to stay longer in bed.

That afternoon he accompanied Rafael and Don Carlos to
a Hebrew service. As they walked along *Jodenbreestreet*, or
Jew Street, he was astonished to see Hebrew lettering openly
displayed above some of the shops. They entered a tall, narrow brick building. Next to the front door was a plaque with a
bronze star of David.

Inside the narrow entrance, an old man with a hunchback
handed them white silk fringed prayer shawls.

One of the recent stowaways, an older man, saw them and
bowed down to Don Carlos in gratitude. With him were a
woman and little girl who went up the staircase to the women's
balcony.

Alfonso followed his father and brother into a large, plain
room with wooden benches and at the front a raised platform,
behind which was a curtained alcove. The men around him
began to chant in Hebrew. He remembered the Jews down by
the docks of Cádiz when he was a child, and he remembered
the woman who had sung such haunting songs on the eve of the
Jews' departure from Spain

The walls of this room were pale gray. The narrow windows
had thick dark panes, and candelabra on the walls blazed with
tiny flames. No images of Madonnas or saints, no fragrance of
burning incense leavened the bareness. The men around him,
as well as those women he had seen on their way to the balcony,
were dressed in severe dark clothing, save for the men's snowy
white prayer shawls with their blue embroidery.

The rabbi opened the curtains behind him and took out a
Torah scroll. He placed it reverently upon a pulpit, unrolled
it, and read from it. A cantor sang a melody, and then the
rabbi began to address the congregation in Flemish.

Alfonso could barely understand the words, but the
rabbi's intensity, and the swaying and moaning of the men
around him as they chanted in response the Hebrew prayers,
affected him strongly. The sea of all their voices rose above

Alfonso's chest and throat until he felt as if he were choking. He leaned his thighs back against the wooden bench and gripped the floor with his feet in order not to fall.

His father, so restrained and courageous in the face of danger, choked back a sob. As Alfonso turned to look at him, he glimpsed the ghost of the old Jew who had tried to abduct him long ago from the wharfs of Cádiz when he was barely seven. The old Jew's white hair and beard floated like a halo around him. He hovered over Don Carlos, who sank to his knees. Rafael and Alfonso tried to pull their father to his feet, but he resisted their efforts.

Let him be, said the old Jew in clear tones. *He has hidden his sorrows, and he needs to mourn.*

Alfonso recalled the Jews clambering onto ships, weeping over their departure from Spain and over the deaths of loved ones. He remembered the ragged Jewish children, their bellies swollen with hunger.

Rafael was still trying to pull their father up, and he seemed not to have heard or seen the ghost, for he looked merely annoyed. *"Come on,"* he whispered before giving up.

However, Don Carlos was not the only one overcome with emotion. Other men's eyes filled with tears as they chanted.

The ghost hovered over them all, then mischievously blew into Alfonso's ear. The ends of his prayer shawl became wings, and he flapped upwards, as he had in Alfonso's childhood dream. He watched the congregation from a spot near the ceiling. But only Alfonso seemed aware of his presence, and he wondered if the Devil were playing tricks upon him.

The service that night contained a *Kol Nidre* prayer, which Don Carlos later explained to Alfonso was a confessional prayer created especially for Marranos. "The words of *Kol Nidre*," said Don Carlos, "mean 'all vows are null and void.' We are all exiled from God in our lives as Marranos. We all need forgiveness. For what we have done, for what we may yet do, we ask pardon for departing from the ways of our ancestors. From now until tomorrow evening we will fast."

How plain the gray room was, how intense the emotions.
From the balcony the women's voices could be heard, higher-
pitched, also laced with cries of suffering.

"Blessed is the Lord our God. For giving us Life. For sus-
taining us. For enabling us to reach this season."

"Hear O Israel the Lord our God, the Lord is One."

Shema Israel Adonai Elohenu, Adonai Ehad.

The room crowded in on Alfonso. He gripped the silk tallit close around his shoulders.

In the following weeks his father and brother taught him
more about Judaism.

He learned that his Hebrew name was Benjamin.

Rafael taught him the Hebrew alphabet and a few words.
He talked about the *Torah* and *Talmud*. He acquainted him
with the writings of Philo, Halevi, Maimonides, and Ibn
Gabirol, who had lived over four hundred years ago and
whose vision of Judaism was so similar to Christianity.
However, what most intrigued Alfonso was a collection of mystical writings which Rafael referred to as *Kabbala*. He himself
had none in his library, as he preferred to study works based
on man's rational faculties.

They discussed different possibilities for Alfonso. He
might join his uncle, Doña Luisa's older brother, Rodrigo, formerly with Cristóbal Colón, who had settled in
Constantinople, where Jews were protected by the Sultan.

Or Alfonso might settle in the north of Spain.

"In those mountains are several towns, filled with people
of stubborn, independent spirit. They're too poor to arouse
the greed of Inquisitors. In these towns, Jews still openly
observe their faith. Not even the queen has been able to sup-
press them."

During those weeks Alfonso developed a taste for the
strong ale they sold in taverns. In addition to Hebrew literature, he was learning about the family shipping business, and
he spent his days in their offices near the wharf. He learned

about cargoes, shipping routes, bills of lading, accounting, and many other practical matters. After the long hours of tedious work, he would frequent the taverns where they sold ale.

Wind blew in from the salt marshes.

Don Carlos gave him a fur-lined cloak and cap to ward off the cold.

He began awakening in the mornings with wet sheets. In sleep, his semen had spilled. Images of Rafael's wife Hannah, half naked, disturbed him. Girls that he passed on the streets as well as the wenches he encountered in taverns stirred his desires, while in his imagination he performed lascivious couplings with them.

When real flesh-and-blood prostitutes beckoned to him from street corners or from the shadows of warehouses, he ignored them.

But he still awakened with sheets damp from semen.

Miguel and his rough companions in Cádiz used to joke about their sexual prowess, and Don Carlos seemed to wink at their deeds.

Nevertheless, Alfonso longed to purge himself of lust. He fasted. He scourged himself with sapling branches as the monks did. He meditated on the Crucifixion as well as on the writings of Maimonides, who had counseled strict discipline of the senses.

CHAPTER 7

They returned to Cádiz in December. To Alfonso, every one in his household seemed different. In their words he heard troubling innuendoes. A sinister mockery seemed to pervade the atmosphere.

The look in Alfonso's eyes frightened his mother, Doña Luisa. He had always been her favorite. When she smoothed his hair affectionately, wanting to talk, he backed away. At meals, he ate no more than a few mouthfuls, and he would stare silently in front of him, not joining the others in conversation.

When he accompanied his family to mass, the Holy Communion wafer tasted bitter. He tried to swallow, but it stuck in his throat. Perhaps the Host had been poisoned. Perhaps the Church knew his secrets.

Bishop Bernardo, with his fox-like face, seemed to look at him strangely.

The Church was enamored of human suffering.

As for Christ who sometimes whispered in Alfonso's ear, was He a demon? Was He merely the product of Alfonso's imagination? Or was the Savior's presence real?

He had an urge to denounce them all, everyone in his family as well as Father Juan. An almost uncontrollable desire seized him to cry out their treachery at the top of his lungs, rousing the swallows from the topmost cornices of the vast domed cathedral.

Candles flickered with golden light. Stained glass windows gleamed in rich tones of red, purple, blue, and green. Stone columns curved through space with exquisite grace. Virgin and Child looked at him sorrowfully. The Son of God hung on His cross with glistening drops of blood on His pearly skin.

"*Cursed be Christ, the bastard son of a menstruating and wanton woman,*" Jews of German lands would taunt their persecutors. Rafael had told him how northern Jews were proud to die "*sanctifying His name.*" Were these stiff-spined people fools or saints?

Just a few words would end all their lives.

"Why not?" whispered a voice. "Why not speak the truth? This world is no more than a vale of tears."

Crumbs of wafer stuck in the back of his throat. Again, he swallowed, and by the utmost effort of will, he kept from choking aloud.

That afternoon he rushed to Father Juan's one-room dwelling behind the cathedral and banged on the door. "You've betrayed me!" he shouted. The vehemence of Alfonso's emotions shocked the priest. It was a cold winter day, and Juan had lit a fire in the stove. A crucifix hung over the priest's bed and a painting of the Madonna and Holy Child graced one wall. Books were heaped on a table. There were two straight-backed chairs. A worn Persian rug covered the tiled floor. Other than that, the small room was bare of furniture. A narrow window looked out onto a courtyard.

"Sit down," he said.

He stared at the fire for a long time in silence, and then spoke, choosing his words carefully. "I have been expecting this visit from you, both dreading and desiring it. Alfonso, I suffered what you are going through now. When I was a child, like you I accepted Christ as the Messiah. The voices of monks in choir used to be heavenly sounds for me. They transported my soul. I still find the music beautiful. But then I saw my relatives slaughtered – your mother's parents – in the Savior's name.

"There is no one in this world I can trust," said Alfonso.

"There is God," said Juan in a low voice.

"Do you make a mockery of Christ?" asked Alfonso angrily "Were you laughing at me all these years?"

"No," said the priest. "I wanted to weep with pity. Your faith was so beautiful. I, too, once possessed that innocent faith. Like you, when I learned that my family was Jewish, I was horrified. Then came the massacres, and after that, I wanted to avenge the wickedness done in Christ's name. Mobs of starving, crazed people led by Dominicans killed infants and children, impaled them on spears, tortured, burned, committed unspeakable acts – after seeing all this, I turned away in revulsion from the Church, and I accepted the path of our common ancestors.

"I have lost all faith," said Alfonso. "I have nothing."

"You still have Jesus. He was what the Jews call a *tzaddik*, a saint, and prophet. The things done in his name would drive him wild with grief. You can still open your heart to his spirit, even if he is not the Messiah."

Alfonso spoke of the night in the marsh. He spoke of his childhood vision of the old Jew and his father praying together and of the miraculous golden threads he found on his pillow that long ago morning. He spoke of how the old Jew reappeared as a ghost in the Amsterdam synagogue. He spoke of Jesus appearing to him in visions.

"Beware of visions, my son. They can lead you dangerously astray. In the end, only God can judge if they're real.

"Rafael has told me about the *Kabbala*. I would like to study it with you," said Alfonso.

"In time," said Juan, gazing into the fire. "But first your spirit must heal. Then we need to use caution. You must be aware that at every step the path of *Kabbala* is a dangerous one.

"Let me tell you a Kabbalistic story. Once upon a time four sages sent their souls up to heaven to gaze on the Divine Light. Its radiance caused the first to die, the second to go mad, the third to become a heretic. Only the fourth, Rabbi Akiba, came back safely. The meaning of the story is clear. The mystical closeness to God that you seek, my child, is fraught with danger.

"You have suffered a severe shock. Give yourself time to
recover. Listen to music. How beautifully your Aunt Silvia
sings! Listen to her songs. Savor food and nature, and exercise
your body. Let time soothe your pain."

They talked for hours, until it was dark outside. Juan
poured red wine. They ate olives and goat cheese. He put more
wood on the fire.

"When I first became a priest and I would raise the Host
during Communion," Juan said, his face flushed with wine, "I
would repeat the words 'this is my body.' I used to fear the
wrath of God because of my hypocrisy. In my heart, I am still
neither fully a Christian nor fully a Jew."

In the following weeks, Alfonso grew closer to Miguel. He
felt pity for this older brother, whom he used to fear and hate.
Their mother, Doña Luisa, had always been colder to Miguel
than to her other sons, and their father did not trust him
enough to tell him their family truth. But beneath Miguel's cal-
lousness, Alfonso perceived a vulnerable spirit.

Alfonso began drinking in the taverns with Miguel and his
companions, riding and jousting with them, practicing swordsmanship, archery, and other warriors' arts.

He was now taller than Miguel, and of a more muscular
build. Thick black hair sprouted on his body. His hands grew
large with long fingers, and his body matured. The mere sight
of a shapely girl would arouse his lust. That disturbed him
deeply, for he still believed in chastity and in original sin.

However, one day he accompanied Miguel's group to
Rosita Pepino's house

"Go on," Miguel said with a smile, as he pushed Alfonso
through a door into a small, bare room. A girl lay there on a
pallet of straw. She had honey-colored skin and long dark
hair. Through the walls he heard a woman's voice and heard a
man's rough laugh. The woman gave a cry, and then she
moaned with pleasure.

"It's his first time," said Miguel to his friends. The others laughed as they slammed the door shut behind Alfonso, and he found himself alone with the girl. She looked no older than Emilia, and she wore a thin white nightdress which barely covered her childish breasts. When Alfonso touched her arm, he felt a child's petal soft skin. She lowered her thick lashes, suddenly shy as she undid the young boy's breeches.

And so it was that he first experienced pleasure with Manuelita, a whore.

Torn as he was between childhood church and still unfamiliar Judaism, his body alone was something certain.

Sometimes as he lay with Manuelita, Emilia's face seemed to interpose itself upon the other girl's. It was her long wavy hair that seemed to cover him, her mouth that sought out his, her body that he caressed.

For Emilia, too, was growing up. Still small, she had her old flashing smile, but she was developing a woman's body. Her black hair hung nearly to her waist. She had a thin face and luminous dark eyes that seemed to see deep inside a person. When he watched the graceful movements of her body beneath the soft, clinging material of the garments that she liked to wear, Alfonso's mind filled with forbidden thoughts.

That spring he broke in a wild mare his father had recently purchased. Each day he would work with the horse in a corral that lay in a grassy field to the west of Cádiz, near the great marshes. The mare was skittish and wild, a two-year old Arabian, pure glistening black with a white cross emblazoned on her forehead.

At the beginning, if anyone approached too closely, she would bare her teeth. The first time he mounted her, she reared and bucked in an effort to throw him. He clung to her flanks with his thighs, bending his body in rhythm with the mare as she bucked. Steadily he reined her in, exerting constant pressure on the bit. His leather hat fell into the dust, which blew into his eyes. Around and around she whirled, trying to shake him. Her mane glistened with sweat, and drops of sweat dripped from Alfonso's face.

Day by day he gently but forcefully put her through her paces. He attached a rope to her harness and trained her, with light touches of the whip, to walk, trot, or gallop in circles around him, according to his command.

He fed her apples and wild oat stalks.

The second time he mounted her, the mare's efforts to throw him were less violent. Gradually, the mare's gait became as smooth as velvet beneath the guidance of his thighs and spurs and his handling of the reins. After he had broken her in, Alfonso spent hours galloping her along the beach, letting the waves and sun and sky as well as the movement fill him, wiping out thoughts.

In March, Miguel embarked on a long sea voyage on one of his father's ships, and Don Carlos sailed for Amsterdam.

One day in early April Doña Luisa said abruptly to Alfonso, "Come with me this afternoon to visit the Duke and Duchess of Cádiz. They are celebrating a feast for Saint Cecilia, which is the Duchess' name day."

At the appointed time, dressed in fine clothing of dark velvet, he walked through the courtyard, still muddy from spring rains, and saw that the carriage had been polished so that it gleamed. The horses had been brushed and curried, their manes adorned with red ribbons.

When he entered the carriage he found only his mother and Emilia inside, also attired in velvet and adorned with jewels. "Where is Aunt Silvia?" he asked. "She couldn't come," said Doña Luisa hastily. As for Inés, he had not expected her to be there, as she had been confined to her bed for weeks with illness.

Alfonso had been at the Duke's palace only several times in his life. He remembered luxurious courtyards and stately rooms flooded with light. "I wonder if there will be music," he said as the carriage jolted over cobblestones. "Of course there will be," said Emilia. "I wore my dancing shoes!" Her eyes met

Alfonso's, and her heart pounded.

Doña Luisa held back her nervousness as they journeyed towards the palace. She sensed the attraction between the two young people, and she felt sympathy for Emilia. As a girl, she had been secretly in love with the priest Juan, her cousin. Although he had feelings for her too, he had a stronger desire to take Holy Orders in order to carry out what he perceived as his mission. What if he had loved her more? What if she had refused to marry Don Carlos, who had been willing to forego a dowry? She savored her moments alone with the priest, when under the guise of confession they talked intimately of matters that would merely have aroused impatience or anger in Don Carlos. The priest's wisdom and compassion were like balm. Although she had grown to love her husband, regrets still haunted her.

When they reached the palace, no other guests were in sight. A servant carrying a lighted torch led them through dark corridors down a stone stairway into a vault decorated with Persian wall hangings. Perhaps fifteen others were gathered there in this windowless, underground space.

The Duchess embraced Doña Luisa with warmth. Alfonso bowed, and Emilia curtsied. Duchess Cecilia was an elegant woman of faded beauty. She wore dark red silk. Diamonds glittered at her ears and throat.

The Duke, surrounded by a group of men, signaled his welcome.

Someone muttered a phrase, and others began to chant in a foreign tongue that sounded like Hebrew. His mother whispered that this was Aramaic, a language even more ancient.

Embroidered white silk *talliot* appeared as if by magic, and Alfonso draped a prayer shawl over himself, following the example of the other men.

The Duke was a grandee, one of those nobles so high in rank that they did not even remove their plumed hats in the presence of the king. He, too, had donned a prayer shawl. Tall

and heavily built, with a light in his eyes, people said he had
enjoyed many mistresses and that women adored him. Rumor
had it that, although he was from an Old Christian family, he
had converted secretly to Judiasm after marrying the
Duchess, who had been born a Jewess.

Alfonso glanced over at Emilia, who had joined the
women on their side of the room. So she, too, had been told
about their Judaism, while Aunt Silvia perhaps remained in
ignorance. He had never spoken with his mother privately
about all this. Truly, walls and even carriage compartments
had ears!

He reflected that in holding this religious service the Duke
and Duchess were risking their lives, their children's lives,
and all they possessed. Suppose Inquisition *familiares* were to
discover them and lock them in this room until the flesh rotted
off their bones?

Father Juan nodded to him from the *bima* or platform in
front of the chamber. He would officiate as rabbi. He was
wearing a *tallit* over a layman's costume of plain dark breeches and tunic.

The ceremony began. It marked the beginning of
Passover.

The Duke removed a stone from the wall. Underneath the
stone was the opening of a wooden door. He unlocked the door
with a key, then took out a tooled-leather box. Inside was the
Torah scroll wrapped in plum-colored velvet.

"It is not only on the eve of Yom Kippur that we atone,"
said Father Juan in a voice that trembled with emotion. "We
also atone on this night, a night of joy which marks our fleeing
from slavery in Egypt. We pray for freedom once again. We
are all transgressors. We are all exiled from God. We are all in
need of forgiveness, because circumstances have forced us to
act with deceit."

The older people sang songs in Hebrew, and the younger
ones tried to follow the words. The melodies lifted them into a
state of joyousness.

After the service they ate hardboiled eggs with lettuce and drank sweet wine.

On the way back from the Duke and Duchess's, all three were silent in the carriage, for even though the coachman could not hear, they dared not speak. Doña Luisa took hold of their hands, and then Emilia and Alfonso grasped each other's. All three, in a closed circle, gripped each other hard.

Emilia now spent hours with the women, engaged in spinning, sewing, weaving, and other work connected with running the household. She no longer studied with Gaillard. She had developed a passion for playing the guitar, and she would play in the evenings. Doña Luisa and Silvia, who both doted on her, didn't have the heart to stop her when she began to neglect household tasks for her music. As for Inés, her daughter's music made her weep with emotion, as it aroused memories of her own youthful dreams. The women realized the intensity of Emilia's need for expression and her hunger for something that lay beyond the world of mundane tasks. Silvia had taught her well, for Emilia, too, had a surprisingly full voice for her small body.

"In the sea there is a tower
In the tower is a girl
Who calls out to passing sailors
Open your window, oh my dove,
I want to climb into your nest ...
Now I lie in my bed above
You beneath a coffin board
Poor trusting boy who died of love"

She would sing this song over and over again. One of Emilia's favorites, the song permeated the household with its haunting melody.

Sometimes, when she sang these romanceros she exaggerated to the point of parody, as if to belie any sentiment of her own. To amuse the household, she would imitate Miguel's

swagger, Silvia's tremulous way of speaking, a servant's clum-
siness. At times her mimicry bordered on cruelty. However, in
Alfonso's presence, she would blush, and her aplomb would
desert her. He had changed so much. There was a quiet certainty about him and an air of power. When he looked at her,
she could feel his desire.

Father Juan had begun to instuct Alfonso in the Kabbala.
"The Kabbala teaches that our dreams are as real as the
waking world," said the priest. "In fact, some Kabbalists say
that waking reality is only a mirage. They say, too, that in our
dreams exist the seeds of the future.

"Kabbalists call God by the name *Ein Sof*, which means
without limits – without end – eternal and infinite. *Ein Sof*
emanates rays of energy called *sephirot*, which permeate the
universe. There are ten principal *sephirot*. Each embodies a
different quality such as mercy and love and judgment, as well
as wisdom.

"Each or our actions – even the flicker of an eyelash –
affects the entire universe, realms above and realms below us.
For each action reverberates, affecting the rhythm and com-
position of the entire universe.

"There are worlds within worlds, infinitely small and infinitely large. They are like mirrors without end.

"Each act of ours, whether or not seen by man, affects
God. And God, *Ein Sof*, is moved to mercy by our own merciful acts. So just as God affects us, we affect God. '*As above, so
below.*'"

Alfonso pondered Juan's words. Contemplating these
beliefs offered a refuge from the inner conflict that was tearing
him apart Although the Kabbala was Judaic, it seemed to exist
on a mountain peak far above the flatlands of either Christian
or Jewish dogma. Kabbala was like a bridge that spanned the
abyss between the two.

Priest Juan usually imparted these teachings when
Alfonso came for confession. They spoke in low voices, always

fearful of being overheard. The priest would actually inspect his quarters before beginning their lesson to make sure no one was hiding anywhere. When either of them wrote down Hebrew letters, Juan was always careful to burn the paper immediately.

"You must carry this knowledge in your head, my child. Even one careless stroke of the quill can bring about your ruin."

Gypsies came to the city. One night they performed their dances in Don Carlos' courtyard. They built a fire in the center and danced around it. Wine poured bountifully.

A gypsy's skirt brushed Alfonso's face as he was resting against cushions. He looked up at her bare calves as she danced. She was full-bodied, her face almost masculine in its strength. The dark, aching sweetness of the woman touched him. Beneath her scarlet skirt billowed many petticoats. Her golden earrings and necklaces gleamed in the light of flames. Her strong fingers beat a rhythm with castanets, while a crowd clapped in rhythm to her steps.

Several servants girls began to imitate the gypsy's steps. Then Emilia joined in. At first she mimicked the dancer. The music stopped. The dancer mopped her brow and sighed, as she sat down to rest. When the musicians started up again, Emilia stood behind other gypsy dancers and imitated their movements, her dark hair falling half over her face. Above one ear she wore a cluster of white jasmine.

One of the male gypsy dancers pulled her towards him. Now she no longer imitated, but she was dancing on her own, while the music filled her body. The singers' voices grew louder. Gypsies clapped in rhythm. An older woman pulled her aside to show her additional dance steps, which Emilia followed. Another woman put castanets around her fingers, and she played, keeping the rhythm as she danced.

A horse whinnied. Then dogs began barking.

When cocks began to crow in the darkness, it was all over,

and the gypsies departed after Don Carlos and the others had
showered them with gold and silver coins for their efforts.
"This one belongs with us," the older woman said, embracing
Emilia, who smiled wistfully.

In the morning, she discovered that her coral earrings
were gone.

Late one evening when almost everyone had gone to bed,
Aunt Silvia strummed her guitar in the moonlit courtyard.

Emilia danced quietly in rhythm to the music. She loved
the suppleness of her own body. She loved the sound of her
voice, as she sang and hummed to the melody. Each dance
movement was a way of thinking out something that she could
not put into words. Slowly and contemplatively she moved,
and as she did, the knotted tangle inside smoothed itself out
into separate threads. She was combing out dark tangles she
could not express in words.

When she thought of Alfonso, she grew almost faint with
desire. At meals, when they sat across from each other at the
long dining table they were magnetized by each other.

And then there was Gaillard! His dashing manner and his
dark, compact handsome looks impressed her. She could not
help laughing at his jokes, even blushing when he touched her
hand. She half-hated him, but his presence stirred her, too.

The music quickened. She danced faster, whirling around
and around, freeing herself of sticky tentacles in her mind.

Hidden in the shadows, the tutor Gaillard watched. He
had drunk far too much wine. What's more, his usual woman
had refused her favors on the pretext of illness, and his lust
had not been satisfied.

He watched Emilia dance. What a morsel she was! That
fine, smooth skin. That elegant body. How enchanting her feet
were with their thin-strapped sandals. He watched the undu-
lation of her hips beneath the billowing white dress. She was
absorbed in her dance as if she were praying. At times her face
relaxed in a languorous smile.

Then as if she sensed his presence, she rushed over to Aunt Silvia and huddled against her.

He waited until the aunt had left. Emilia walked slowly through the courtyard and along the walkway bordered by columns in the Roman style. She was deep in thought, moving in a half-trance, as she went back towards her room.

She climbed the stairs. "*Emilia, ma douce,*" whispered Gaillard, when she reached the landing, which was entirely dark. Emilia gave a start. Ah, he knew that he excited her, too. He grabbed her around the waist, cupping his hands beneath her breasts.

She screamed and tried to pull away. Her screams echoed against the stones. When he clapped one hand over her mouth, she bit down hard. People came running. Servants, masters in nightclothes, carrying lighted candles and torches.

"Let her go!" The point of Don Carlos' sword jabbed Gaillard's spine.

Emilia ran off, sobbing.

The sword jabbed again and again lightly at his spine, piercing through his clothes.

"Get out of my house!" thundered Don Carlos

Amid wailing and crying of women, Gaillard packed his few belongings and his books into a sack and fled into the darkness.

The next morning Don Carlos summoned Emilia to his study. "You will go to the Convent of Santa Carmen," he said. "I should have sent you long ago. You will remain there until we arrange a suitable marriage. I will give you a dowry."

"No!" she cried. "I don't want to leave. Why are you punishing me for Gaillard's wickedness?"

"This is not a punishment. The convent will give you the skills and polish of a lady. A young girl like you is a source of temptation. I've dismissed Gaillard, leaving Alfonso without a tutor. He, too, is bearing the consequences of Gaillard's actions."

"Please let me stay!"

He was unmoved.

She ran out of his study, sobbing uncontrollably, and locked herself in her room. Inés brought her trays of food, but Emilia refused to eat.

Grieving for her daughter, Inés also pleaded with Don Carlos to let her daughter stay at home. She herself had grown weak and suffered from mysterious fainting spells. She had aged greatly, and her hair had turned white. Falling to her knees, she begged him to relent. But Don Carlos remained adamant. He would consent only to a fortnight's delay.

Under the pressure of her impending departure, Alfonso and Emilia arranged to meet in a chapel that lay deep within the labyrinthian chambers of the Cathedral. There they at last spoke of their feelings for each other. They embraced, savoring each other's closeness. He kissed her soft lips. Tears ran down her cheeks. Then she pulled away abruptly.

"Alfonso, are you still seeing Manuelita?"

"She's pregnant," he said, unwilling to hold this back.

"How do you know you're the father?"

"I don't know, although she swears I am."

Emilia shuddered. "What are you going to do?"

"I'll see to it that she and the baby are provided for. I'll arrange for peasants to raise the child."

"Alfonso, promise you won't see her any more!"

"I can't do that," he said. "She's human, after all, and she's pregnant."

It was common practice for young noblemen to learn the arts of love with girls like those at Rosita Pepino's house. For such girls, it was a source of pride to bear a nobleman's child. Although the image of Alfonso and Manuela lying naked in each other's arms tormented her, there was a severity in his voice that forbade her from pursuing the subject.

In the dim light of the votive candles, Emilia made him think of a dusky madonna. She wore an indigo dress of fine cotton, embroidered with silver. But she looked so sad.

He drew her close again. He could feel the pounding of

her heart in her bony ribs beneath her breasts, and he smelled the jasmine fragrance that she wore. "Emilia, when I lay with her, I used to imagine I was with you."

"Do you love her?"

"No, I pity her."

"I don't want to share you with anyone."

"Emilia, it's you I love, and I always have. I want to spend my life with you."

She held him tightly and buried her face against his shoulder.

He lifted her face toward his. "Emilia, will you marry me?"

"Yes," she murmured.

They prayed together on their knees in front of the Virgin in her niche.

Then Emilia turned to him, and in her face he read questions about how much he was truly Christian or Jew, questions which neither of them dared utter aloud, even if they believed themselves to be entirely alone here. This was a topic even more dangerous than their secret love.

In the morning, the women of the household tearfully hugged her goodbye. They gave her hampers of food and embroidered keepsakes. Then Emilia, accompanied by her mother and the coachman, left for a convent near Seville.

CHAPTER 8

*"One of the reasons for circumcision is to bring about a
decrease in sexual intercourse and a weakening of the organ . . . the
bodily pain caused to that member is its real purpose . . . circumcision . . . weakens the faculty of sexual excitement and perhaps
sometimes diminishes its pleasure. . . . Who first began to perform
this act if not Abraham, who was celebrated for his chastity?*

*"Circumcision has another meaning . . . those who believe in
the unity of God should have a bodily sign uniting them. . . . Now a
man does not perform this act upon himself or a son unless it be in
consequence of a genuine belief . . . it . . . is a very, very hard thing."*

– Maimonides, *Guide to the Perplexed.*

Eight members of the Castro family were arrested by the
Inquisition. They were said to be Marranos. Grand-
parents, parents, even the two older children, who were eleven
and thirteen were all thrown into prison. The three youngest
were placed under the care of nuns at the Carmelite Convent,
as if they were already orphans.

It was whispered that Don Luis Castro had secretly circumcised himself.

People said *familiares* had come at night and seized all
members of the family as they lay sleeping, that they had been
betrayed by a servant, and that *familiares*, dressed in black,
had taken them in chains to prison.

The Castro family lived in a large house only a few blocks
from theirs. Señor Castro had been a tax collector. The family owned estates in the country with olive and almond and
orange groves. All the Castro properties – all their houses and
lands – were now seized by the Church.

One day shortly after their arrests, as Alfonso walked

along the cobblestone streets, a perception of strangeness came over him. The sky was clear azure. A dog barked. A raven flew high above, circling just to the north above the Guadalquivir River. *This world is only a mirage. What is real lies in our dreams.* Kabbalists believed reality to exist in the realm of dreams. But during these last nights, his dreams had been filled with terror. *Beneath the black letters of the Torah on white parchment lies an invisible text, wherein all is reversed. There white flames dance on black fire. The visible Torah is only a garment covering its body. So outward reality is only a garment that covers the truth within.* These sayings perplexed and yet comforted him. As he walked, all the physical world – the sky, the trees, the dog barking, the raven flying, the narrow street shadowed by buildings – seemed to be a deceptive covering.

A mood of anxiety floated like a sea all around them. Alfonso's family feared their own servants. He wondered what had become of Gaillard, and if the former tutor knew their secret and would betray them.

One night his mother talked to him about Emilia. "If you love each other, then marry her," she said quietly, as she spun white wool. It was one of the rare times they were alone together. "I loved Juan when I was a girl. He loved me, too, but he loved the priesthood more. His family put great pressure on him to become a priest, so that he could help others carry on." Her voice trailed off. Alfonso nodded.

"Don Carlos does not understand." She snapped off the thread and took the white skein off its spindle, then put it into a straw basket beside the spinning wheel. "In the end, I grew to love him. Your father is a good man and a loving husband. But for you I want . . . I want you to follow your heart. . . ." Her voice trailed off, the silence filled with words she dared not say.

Church bells sounded through the evening air.

He still made love to Manuela, and he suffered over this

and did penance by murmuring countless *Ave Marías* and *Paternosters* on his beads. Although he only half believed in their efficacy, they gave Alfonso some satisfaction, rooted as they were in his childhood.

"Sexual love between a man and woman can be a way of approaching God," Father Juan said unexpectedly one day. They were sipping wine during Alfonso's lesson. "The *Shekhinah*, the Divine Presence which watches over our people, is drawn like a moth to a flame when two people's bodies and souls connect in love."

"Is that what Moses of León wrote in the *Zohar*?" asked Alfonso. They had been going over the thirteenth century kabbalist's famous writings, purportedly channeled by an ancient spirit of Safed in the Holy Land.

"Yes, he did – or his guiding spirit did," said the priest. "On the other hand, sexual union where there is a lack of love harms the soul."

Alfonso avoided the priest's gaze. He did not want to discuss his desire for Manuela. Increasingly, he wanted to keep his distance from the priest. He wanted to discover guidance within himself.

Manuela had grown lustrous with pregnancy. Her eyes, her copper ringlets, and her skin gleamed. She would wait for him on a street corner near the docks where she lived, timidly pull at his sleeve, and like a lamb, he would go with her. Her belly was swelling with her fifth month of pregnancy. Soon they would no longer be able to make love without endangering the baby. (Was it really his, as she swore?)

Perhaps he should circumcise himself, like Don Luis Castro. Perhaps then he would be able to master his lust. People said Don Luis had used a surgeon's knife, that he had nearly died, and that a servant who glimpsed the grievous wound had told Inquisitors in exchange for a sum of gold.

A mad idea! The Devil had insinuated himself deep within his mind.

Miguel returned from an eighteen months voyage to the Orient around Cape Horn, toughened by experience. He worked as first mate on their father's ship, *Santa Carmen*, and had even helped the captain put down a mutiny at sea, although some said he had been too harsh. And he had carried out highly successful negotiations, coming back with a fortune in silks, sandalwood, ivory, and spices.

There was a curious cold glitter about him. His gray-blue eyes were more scrutinizing. He was even thinner and more sinewy than he had been, as well as a little taller.

A few days after his return, he suggested that Don Carlos and Alfonso accompany him for a ride in the country. Unaccompanied by servants, they rode out beyond the city gates. They galloped along the road and then along paths that wound through vineyards and groves of budding olive trees. The air smelled fresh.

They stopped to rest by the river, dark muddy-green, rushing with the water of spring rains, and they tethered their horses, letting them graze on the tender new flowering branches. They drank wine from a goatskin flask.

Miguel cut thin slices of codfish with swift, violent movements. "It's a good thing we didn't bring pork." His voice had a strange tone. "We rarely eat it at home, and Mother usually manages to be sick when we do." He looked around to make sure no wandering peasant or shepherd was within earshot.

"In Bombay a Jew approached me," he said, looking levelly at Don Carlos, with that same strange tone to his voice. "He congratulated me on being the son of a man so loyal to his people. Then he knelt and kissed my feet in gratitude to you for saving his life."

Don Carlos stared straight ahead.

"He told me how you smuggle Jews out of our land. He said that he'd seen you with your two sons in a synagogue in Amsterdam, and he had thought I was one of them."

"Evidently, he was mistaken," said Don Carlos, his voice dry as gravel.

"Why did you never tell me?" Miguel's pointed, intense face was drawn with emotion. His voice grew louder. "Why was I left out of the family secret? It's obvious that you don't trust me. Yet I am the cleverest of your sons by far when it comes to trading. This mad monk, Alfonso, here has no interest in it. As for Rafael, he's hidden himself away in Amsterdam, and you've managed to keep me at a safe distance."

"Miguel . . ." Don Carlos moved forward as if to touch him, but Miguel backed off.

"As you know better than anyone else, when you've drunk too much you say things that are better left unsaid, and you commit actions that you later regret. I feared your quarrelsome temper as well as the company you keep. Perhaps I was mistaken not to tell you. It would have been better for you to hear this from me than from a stranger."

Miguel stared at him impassively.

Don Carlos' voice trembled. "By tradition, *anusim*, the ones like our ancestors who were forced to convert under threat of death, reveal their true faith only to the oldest sons, who in turn pass it on under the protective covering of Holy Orders. As ecclesiastics, these men can study Hebrew without arousing suspicion. But Rafael wanted to marry. So I chose Alfonso to carry on. Because of his mystical leanings, I thought him suited to become a priest"

"I've always been an outsider in our family," Miguel said bitterly. "I'm the black sheep. Good for gaining worldly riches, but not for much else."

Alfonso ached for his brother. "At first I was sick at heart and angry when I learned the truth," he said to Miguel. "I felt betrayed. I thought Jews were monsters, possessed by the Devil. All the stories I'd heard as a child about how Jewish men bled like women and had tails like beasts lodged deep within me."

"Your Aunt Silvia doesn't know, nor does her son Diego," said Don Carlos. "It is far too dangerous to tell more than a few in a family."

Miguel plunged his knife furiously into the ground.

"I'm the son who can salvage your fortune and your lives. Don't you realize that at any moment the Inquisition is likely to throw the lot of you – and me – into prison. If Jews in Bombay know about us, you may be sure that many other people also do. You're like a man perched with one foot on a perilous ledge."

"I trust in God," said Don Carlos

"I have no such exalted faith. Even when I was a child, the Church did not impress me. Alfonso, I used to wonder how you could kneel in front of your little altar for hours on end. I thought you were a fool, taking refuge in some kind of magic that I did not believe in. What I'm saying now, I'm well aware, would endear me to the *familiares* no less than your Judaizing."

A shaft of sunlight lit the small golden earring that hooped through his left ear. He looked around once more to make sure no one had come within earshot, then spoke in a low, impassioned voice.

"Father, all of you should leave Spain immediately. Take only a few servants you trust. Take your gold, your jewels. We can oversee our affairs from Constantinople or Salonika, or the famous Amsterdam you arranged for me not to visit. Any of these cities are safer."

"I have powerful friends who will protect us."

"No one protected the Castro family."

"We haven't done anything as outrageous as Don Luis has in circumcising himself. The Duke of Cádiz. is my friend."

"You mean he is *one of you*," said Miguel, with a sneer. "He can do nothing, and he's now away at the Royal Court in Madrid."

"My roots are in Spain," said Don Carlos. "I have a mission, which I cannot accomplish if I leave. I was born here, and God willing, I'll die here."

"You help others reach safe lands, yet you refuse to help

yourself and your family," said Miguel, violently cutting the codfish into smaller pieces with his hunting knife. No one had any appetite for eating the white morsels.

A rabbit scurried in front of them. Within the blink of an eye, Miguel had speared the creature, and they watched it writhe piteously beneath his knife. Blood oozed from the wound. "You're like the rabbit," said Miguel coldly. "You're waiting to be killed."

He plunged the knife deeper, until the creature made a last convulsive movement and lay still.

They rode back perturbed, all of them. Don Carlos galloped on ahead, furious and agitated.

Alfonso rode alongside his brother. "Let's race to the top of that hill," he said, to divert Miguel from his gloomy thoughts He pointed out a path to the right that crossed a meadow and cut through a wooded slope.

Miguel reined in his horse, a frisky gelding. "We'll start here," he said. Alfonso patted the neck of the mare he had trained and held her back while she chomped at the bit.

They galloped abreast, then Alfonso's mare pulled ahead as the path narrowed through the woods. Miguel lashed out with his whip, flicking the mare's rump. She reared and bucked, nearly throwing Alfonso, then intensified her speed. A length ahead, his mare reached the crest, where there was a clearing. He halted, turned his horse around, and raised one arm up in the air in a gesture of victory.

Miguel approached very close on his horse, then suddenly withdrew his sword and placed its cold steel blade against Alfonso's neck.

"Go on, kill me," said Alfonso, feeling an unreal calm. He looked his brother in the eyes. "Go ahead."

On Miguel's face was a strange expression. Alfonso kept looking at his brother, feeling the force of his gaze affect Miguel. Then suddenly Miguel hurled his sword to the ground. "You're my *brother*," he said in a choked voice.

Later by the banks of the flowing river beneath willow

trees, they talked while their horses nibbled on spring grass.
Alfonso related what he had learned of their family's past. As
the sun sank lower in the sky, he ventured to speak a little
about the *Kabbala.*

"These kabbalistic ideas are only the products of men's
imagination," said Miguel. "You're a dreamer. What is real for
me is the earth, the sea, the sun and moon and stars, and the
flesh of a woman. In Bombay I used to visit a house where the
young girls were as exquisite as almond blossoms. The pleasures they gave me were worth all your *Kabbala."*

"However," said Alfonso, "These pleasures now exist only
in your memory. They're short-lived."

"Moment's of joy are worth a lifetime of thoughts!
Alfonso, why don't you sail with me on my next trip and see
something of the world before you abandon it for God. All of
you are living like terror-stricken dogs with your tails between
your legs – and with good cause."

During the days that followed, Don Carlos closeted himself in his study with Miguel and had long talks with him, trying to repair the rift. Miguel asked his father to let him captain
one of his ships. Despite misgivings, Don Carlos finally agreed
to do so, provided that his son study privately with Father
Juan until Pentecost and that he reflect on his past actions in
order to master his impulses. Furthermore, impressed with
Miguel's business acumen, he taught him all that he could
about the family business, so that Miguel might be able to take
on more responsibilities from abroad.

For her part, Doña Luisa also softened towards Miguel
and was more affectionate with him than usual.

However, one night he came home with a knife wound in
his thigh after a drunken brawl. "He needs to be fighting
pirates or savages," said Don Carlos, deeply discouraged.
When this son of theirs was angry or drunk, God alone knew
what he might say or do.

CHAPTER 9

Inés grieved over Emilia's absence. She had asked little of life, except that her daughter flourish. When she had journeyed with Emilia to the convent, the bleakness of the place disheartened her. Her lovely blossom Emilia would wilt, she feared, in those surroundings.

Her own health had been frail over the past few years. Now she could no longer hold food and she had lost a great deal of weight. The physician said a tumor was choking off her bodily functions. She was dying.

Emilia was summoned home from the convent. She and Doña Luisa spent long hours at her mother's bed, seeing to it that Inés was never unattended. They applied warm compresses to her belly and groin and rubbed her cold feet to keep them warm. Doña Luisa told stories to entertain her, and Emilia would sing to her.

Inés had so much that she wanted to tell her daughter about their family's past, about the father she had never known, about her own life, and about her own yearnings which had never been fulfilled. She had so much to say, yet so little time, and she was growing weak, and it was hard to find the right words, still harder to express things that lay beneath the realm of words.

At the end, Emilia refused even to let Doña Luisa attend her, and she would not leave her mother's side, often holding her mother's hand, and sleeping barely at all.

Inés began to have difficulty breathing. Her skin took on a gray tone. They called in a young peasant girl who was said to have healing power, but she lacked the strength of the *ensalmador* who had saved Emilia's life and who had perished in the *auto da fé.*

Father Juan administered Extreme Unction.

In a barely audible voice, Inés asked the servants to leave, and she turned her face to the wall and muttered the words of the *Shema.*

"Hear oh Israel the Lord our God, the Lord is one."

Emilia fell to her knees and prayed aloud, "Dear Jesus and Mary, let her live." But then she silently prayed to the God of Israel. *

Two days later Emila stood in the dark hallway outside her mother's empty room. She and Doña Luisa had prepared Inés for burial, but Emilia could sense her mother's presence as she clutched her mother's amulet between her breasts. This was the silver amulet Inés always wore around her neck and that Alfonso had given her mother long ago, when he was only a child. She also wore her mother's garnet earrings and her blue silk shawl.

She thought of the convent with its narrow beds covered with white linen, all in a row. Convent bells ringing. Convent prayers. Once a week they washed themselves in cold water from the well, a little at a time, so that the body would not be immodestly exposed.

At night a little girl named Béatriz, would climb into her bed, huddling next to Emilia for warmth and comfort. Because Béatriz' family could no longer afford to pay her keep, the nuns now treated her harshly. What hypocrites they were, with their talk of Christian love and charity.

When they placed the casket in the earth and began to shovel dirt over it, Emilia began to scream. She heard herself crying out and sobbing, as if her desperate cries came from another entity inside her "She's not dead! You're burying her alive!" In her mind Emilia saw her mother pound at the walls of her coffin, as in ghost stories. Perhaps her mother was still alive but was suffocating for lack of air! She flung herself upon the coffin, screaming and crying out, "She's alive! She's alive!"

People pried her hands away from the edges of the coffin and carried her off, while she kept on screaming, "Mami! Mami!"

For days she would not eat or speak to anyone. She stayed in her room, and she drank only a few sips of water that someone had placed in a silver cup by her bed.

She dimly recalled Alfonso appearing beside her bed, and she felt embarrassed to be in a worn nightgown, her hair matted, her body foul-smelling with sweat and sorrow. "Cheer up, little bird," he said. He held her close, murmuring words of love.

After he had left, she walked to the window, opened the curtain, and looked out onto the courtyard where flowers bloomed in brilliant color. When Aunt Silvia brought her the guitar, she strummed it and sang, soothing herself with the music.

"By the sea there is a tower
In the tower is a girl
Who calls out to passing sailors...
Oh my dove, I lie in my bed above.
You beneath a coffin board
Poor trusting one who died of love"

Aunt Silvia and Doña Luisa bathed Emilia in lavender water. They dressed her in clean clothing, brushed her hair, gently led her down the stairs, their arms around her, and induced her to sit at the long table with everyone else.

Alfonso sat next to her and gripped her hand. "Emilia, *mi amor*," he said in a low voice. The gentleness in his voice and the look in his eyes made Emilia burst into tears again. Despite the fact that people surrounded them, he drew her close and kissed her forehead.

"I love Emilia, and I want to marry her," he said in a

clear voice, addressing his father, who sat at the head of the
table.

Emilia clenched her fingers hard against her palms.

Don Carlos revealed no emotion as he passed a platter of
venison to Aunt Silvia. "The meat is done to a turn," he said.

Later that evening Alfonso formally asked his father's
consent. They were in Don Carlos' study. Outside cicadas
sounded, and the fragrance of *dama de nocha* wafted through
the open window, while Alfonso could scarcely breathe as he
waited for Don Carlos to break the silence. His father picked
up his quill pen and twirled it, then placed it down upon a
blank parchment.

"I've made plans for you to enter the priesthood," he
said.

"I don't want to be a priest. I love Emilia."

"Her mother was a servant," said his father.

"She was Mother's friend."

"Only through our kindness."

"Emilia is my equal in grace and sensibility and breed-
ing."

"Hugo, the cloth merchant's son, has asked for her hand.
I've agreed to provide a dowry." He put down the quill.
"There's nothing more to discuss."

Alfonso looked at his father with pure hatred.

"I'll kill myself before I marry Hugo," said Emilia. It was
her last evening in Cádiz. She and Alfonso were standing
together in the upper courtyard, watching the birds in the
aviary. She had begged Don Carlos to let her return to the
convent for a period of mourning, and he had consented. She
was to leave at dawn.

"I'll take nuns' vows first, although I have no desire to
live my life in a convent."

"We could run away and marry secretly," whispered
Alfonso.

"No," she muttered. "I need time to grieve for my mother. Besides, I don't want a furtive marriage. I want to be married with dignity and honor."

They watched as the canaries, doves, and other species of birds flew about inside their cages, circling, hovering, preparing to roost in the coming darkness. Their yellow and green and orange-hued wings filled the air.

"I'll sleep with a knife under my pillow. If they try to take me away from the convent, they'll take my corpse."

"No, Emilia," he whispered, drawing her close. "I'll make my father accept you."

"Oh Alfonso, I'm so afraid." She bit her lip. "What about Manuelita? Will you see her when I'm gone?"

"She's bearing my child."

"I don't want you to see her."

"She's a pitiful girl, a prostitute. Her mother abandoned her at birth. Rosita Pepino is the only mother she has ever known."

"You're fond of her."

"Emilia, it's not right to speak of the two of you in the same breath! Let's not spoil our last evening together with bitter words."

He pressed her against a column, hungrily kissed her, and she responded, barely able to withstand the intensity of her sensations. She felt transported, as if she would float right out of her body, so delicious was it to hold and be held. She longed to take him to her room and to make love with him, but that could not be.

A month later Manuela gave birth to a healthy baby boy, and Don Carlos toasted Alfonso with a group of companions. "To Alfonso and to his first-born son – may he father many more!"

But Alfonso was not there. He had sailed for Egypt with Miguel.

CHAPTER 10

Cádiz, Winter 1501-1502

They were bound for Alexandria on one of his father's ships with its cargo of oranges, almonds, wines, olives, and cedar wood.

Miguel was captain, and Alfonso, in the capacity of an ordinary seaman, was beginning to learn navigation. Two days out at sea, Miguel caught a cabin boy stealing a bottle of port from his private quarters. He gave the youth a blow that sent him reeling against the wall.

Miguel demanded that the crew watch him administer a flogging to the boy, who had been bound naked with ropes to the forward mast. Again and again Miguel lashed out with his leather whip until blood poured down the boy's back. The whip furrowed deep into the boy's flesh. He was only twelve or thirteen, slender, dark-skinned, with an innocent face. His cries rang out, while the seamen's anger burned in their faces.

Finally the boy sagged unconscious against the mast.

Miguel's lash again came down.

"Stop! You'll kill him!" Alfonso cried, planting himself squarely in front of his brother.

"Get out of my way!" shouted Miguel.

Alfonso tore the whip from Miguel's hands and hurled it over the deck.

"Take my brother away," commanded Miguel.

Alfonso did not resist when the First and Second Mate grabbed hold of his arms and roughly led him below deck, throwing him face first into a dank, stinking hole of a prison beneath the forecastle. He landed half on a narrow straw pal-

let, half on filthy flooring. When he got to his feet, the ceiling
was so low that he could not stand upright. Then he crouched
down on the pallet, and he tried to close out the horrid smells
and his physical discomfort by closing his eyes and focusing on
light, on Hebrew letters that conveyed power and meaning in
their shapes and in their sounds. But he was wretched, and his
throat was parched.

Many hours passed before Alfonso heard a key turn in the
lock. The door creaked open, and as the ship rolled with
heavy waves, Alfonso saw his brother, stern and pale, illu-
mined by the lantern he was holding. A shiver ran through
Alfonso. He had a sense of having lived this moment before,
and he also had a sense of foreboding, as if this were an omen.

Miguel's face was grim. "Come with me," he said. The
ship was rolling hard. When they ascended to the deck,
Alfonso swallowed gulps of fresh air. A harsh wind was blowing. High waves were pitching the ship, and the sails bellied
out. Clouds covered the sky. But when they parted, they
revealed a nearly full moon which shone on everything, giving
an eerie glow to the mast, the sails, the outlines of the ship and
of sleeping sailors. Alfonso, unsteady on his feet after his con-
finement, struggled to keep his balance as he followed Miguel
to the stern and down the ladder to the captain's cabin.

There he sat on the edge of the bunk while Miguel seated
himself on a stool beside his small table, which held a quill
pen, a leather-bound log, and other papers.

"You defied my authority in front of the sailors," said
Miguel. He drank deeply from a leather flask of rum, and then
passed it to Alfonso, who refused.

"You haven't earned it," said Alfonso. "Such cruelty
demeans you," said Alfonso, his stomach hollow from lack of
food or drink over many hours, yet queasy from the motion of
the ship.

"The boy deserved his punishment."

"Why were you so violent with him?"

"He wasn't only stealing my liquor. Look at this!" said Miguel, shoving a crumpled piece of paper into Alfonso's hand.

When Alfonso spread it out, he saw a crude charcoal drawing of a pig and the word "Marrano" scrawled in block letters.

"I found this on the floor. I think he meant to leave it here," said Miguel.

"Then we're doomed," muttered Alfonso.

"Only fools are doomed! We'll sail on from Alexandria to Constantinople and visit our uncle Rodrigo, who is a wealthy man and may help us."

"I'm going home as soon as I can," said Alfonso, thinking of Emilia.

"You'd be crazy to go back. Our parents have known all along they're a hairsbreadth from the Inquisitor's prison."

During the rest of the voyage, a pall hung over the ship.

The cabin boy survived, his shoulder crippled by the beating. There were murmurs on the part of the crew against Miguel. But for the most part they both feared and respected their captain.

When they dropped anchor in the port of Algiers, where they were to unload part of the cargo and replenish supplies, Alfonso bade his brother farewell and booked passage home on a Greek ship.

Six days later Alfonso arrived in Cádiz. Foreboding assailed him through this return voyage, and he would awaken in a sweat to the sounds of cries ringing in his ears. Yet all around him it was silent, except for the rocking of waves against the sides of the vessel.

It was late in the afternoon when he made his way home. As the porter's mule lopped along the cobblestones, his sense of disaster grew stronger. The drawing of the pig was a warning! He should not be coming home at all. But he *had* to. He could not abandon Emilia, and he realized now that he could

not abandon his family either. Perhaps he should have sent a
messenger on ahead to ascertain the situation at home.
However, a sense of fatality as well as a strange lassitude ruled
his actions.

At last he pounded on their heavy iron knocker.

Next door a dog barked. He pounded a second time, shivering in the cold, fearing the silence. Where was Vanno, their
doorkeeper? At last he heard boots sound out against the floor
tiles. "Who's there?"

"Alfonso."

Slowly their major-domo, Pedro, a balding, elderly man
dressed in his usual black with white ruffled shirt front and
cuffs, opened the door. Pedro had been in their service since
before Alfonso's birth.

The mule driver carried his trunk inside. After Alfonso
had paid him and he had driven off in his cart, old Pedro
pulled Alfonso into the doorkeeper's chamber, which was
empty, and stared at him in silence, his eyes anguished, evidently searching for words.

"What's happened?" asked Alfonso. "Where's Vanno?"

"He's gone. Half the servants have fled." The major-
domo's voice echoed against the walls.

"Why?"

The house was eerily quiet, except for a burst of sudden,
shrill laughter. Alfonso waited to hear what he already knew.

"Three nights ago *familiares* came to the house. They
seized your mother, your father, and your aunt."

Kabbalists wrote of cause and effect. A flutter of an eyelash causes ripples throughout an infinity of worlds. Miguel's
cruelty and his loss of temper had created a cataclysm. The
passage of time was an illusion. One's actions could affect the
past as well as the future. This moment had been marked out
long ago. Now he, Alfonso, coincided with it, just as loaded
dice lands on a gaming table.

"Señor, you cannot stay here," said Pedro. "It's too dangerous. Very few of the servants can be trusted. I advise you to

leave at dawn for Cordoba." In a lower voice he added, "It's best if I don't know where you've gone."

Pedro stooped and lifted up a corner floor tile. Underneath it lay a metal box. He put it on the table, and slowly he took off the lid. Inside were half a dozen large, rusted house keys.

"Jews left these with your father years ago. They thought that one day they would return."

Alfonso picked up the keys and held them in his hands. Each key told a sad tale. Then he carefully placed them back inside the box.

"What shall I do with them, Señor?"

"Put them back where they were. Perhaps a miracle will take place," said Alfonso, thoroughly disheartened.

Just then one maid called out to another, their voices echoing as freely as if they were outside in the fields.

The major-domo led Alfonso through a back passageway to the kitchen, where Teresa, who had been his wet-nurse long ago and now served as cook, was stirring a pot on the stove. When she saw Alfonso she dropped her wooden spoon, burst into tears, and hugged him to her thick bosom as if he were still a child.

"My poor Alfonso," she sobbed. "My poor boy!"

She served him a bowl of codfish soup, bread, and wine. Famished as he was, he consumed the meal hungrily.

Then Pedro led him up the back stairs and through dark hallways, motioning Alfonso to halt when they heard a slight noise. A shadowy woman's figure, skirts rustling, crossed the hallway in front of them. After waiting a moment, they walked swiftly past the door through which she had gone.

They reached the outdoor bird patio. Although it was night by now and stars gleamed above, the birds were flying wildly about inside their cages, chirping louder than usual, as if it were still daylight and as if they sensed catastrophe.

The major-domo brought Alfonso hot water for washing, prepared his bed with clean linen, laid out fresh clothes, then left. Alfonso fell to his knees in front of the little cedar altar in which he had prayed as a child. But when he prayed to Jehovah, Jesus, and finally the Christian God, he sensed no Holy Presence, only a vast, frightening void. Jesus was distant as the stars.

CHAPTER 11

In his troubled sleep, Alfonso dreamed of black crows circling over a dead man in a field. When he awakened, it was still dark. He quickly dressed and went to the stable to saddle his mare.

As he was tightening the girth, the mare suddenly neighed and reared, tearing loose from his grip. He turned around. In the dim light that came through the open door, he saw three men dressed entirely in black, their faces half concealed by scarves, One of them clamped his large hand over Alfonso's nose and mouth, so that he could scarcely breathe. The others bound his hands and feet with hemp cords, then threw him into the back of a cart. As the cart drove off, his horse kept on neighing wildly, as if she sensed what was happening.

He scarcely felt the jolting of the cart over cobblestones. He was in shock, his mind and body paralyzed with fear. Who had betrayed him? Was it Pedro, the major domo? A spying servant?

The *familiares*, for that is who they were, carried him inside a building, then flung him down onto a hard floor. Their receding footsteps sounded against the stone surface.

A guard in gray breeches and brown tunic appeared and looked down at Alfonso. He had a round face and small blue eyes.

"Where am I?" asked Alfonso.

The guard did not reply, as he unbound Alfonso. Then he gave him a shove, crying "Get up!"

Dazed and aching, Alfonso followed the guard through windowless hallways lit by wax tapers . They entered a room with polished tile floors and Persian carpets. Light streamed in through arch-shaped window, bordered by blood red curtains. A cleric in black Dominican robes sat at a mahogany table.

Alfonso rubbed his hands, which were raw where the hemp cords had cut into them. The Dominican looked ominously familiar, but Alfonso could not place him.

The thought of his mare neighing and rearing up with fright came to him. Who would care for her now? Had the Inquisitors sequestered all his family's property? Would Miguel, too, fall into their snares?

To the right of the Dominican stood a white flag with the green cross of the Inquisition. To his left stood the flag of Jesus the Savior, a white cross on a field of blue. On the wall above the cleric hung a handsome ebony crucifix with an emaciated Christ.

"Alfonso Valdez, do you know why we've brought you here?" asked the Dominican in a surprisingly gentle voice.

"No, Señor."

"You're here to answer questions, my son. If you answer truthfully and fully, you have nothing to fear."

Out of the corner of his eye, Alfonso saw one of the guards smirk ever so slightly.

"Are my parents here? Where is my aunt Silvia."

"That's not your concern!" Gesturing to two guards, burly men in ragged breeches, vests, and shirts, he ordered them to take Alfonso away.

"I'll give you time to rest and reflect. Tomorrow we'll question you."

The guards led him up a flight of stairs and along a corridor that overlooked a courtyard. They walked through a gallery of fine paintings of religious subjects and of noble families. Finally, the guards led him into a large bedroom which had brown velvet draperies, a bed, a table-desk, and a chair. In the corner was a stand with a bowl for washing, along with a pitcher of water.

The guards locked the door behind them.

Alone, he pulled aside a drape. The window behind it was barred. It overlooked the street. He wondered what family the house had formerly belonged to. Where were they now? Was this the former house of the Mendez family, who had been fortunate enough to escape long ago?

He looked up at the ceilings. They were high and arched. Could someone be spying down on him through a peephole, or peering through a crack in one of the walls? Although he was alone, he had the sensation that he was being watched. He sat down at the table and closed his eyes. Hebrew letters blazed white inside his inner eyes. White flames on black velvety air. Black flames devouring the white letters.

His head ached.

The bed had a crucifix at its head. He knelt down and prayed to both Jesus and J-H-V-H. Once again, he had the vision of the Hebrew letters. This time they circled Our Lord as he danced among the white flames in a black night, blood pouring from his side, a white rag around his loins.

"Jesus help me," he said aloud.

"God help me." *Shema Israel Adonai Elohenu, Adonai Ehad* . . . Hear Oh Israel the Lord our God, the Lord is One," he added silently, afraid even to whisper the Hebrew words aloud for fear of an invisible witness.

He heard a key turn in the lock. His door opened, and a thin youth dressed in black put a tray on the table. "For the Marrano," he said, gazing directly at Alfonso. Then he left, locking the door behind him.

The silver tray contained a pitcher of water, hard bread, and a plate of olives.

Alfonso knew he should eat to keep up his strength, but he had no appetite. When he tried to swallow a bit of olive, it stuck in his mouth, and he felt he would choke until he spit it out.

Finally he lay down on the bed with its brocade coverlet, and he fell into a troubled sleep, with nightmares so vivid that he thought he was awake.

Then someone was shaking him. He opened his eyes, and he realized he had been dreaming. Was he still dreaming, or was this real? The guard with the round face and small blue eyes was peering down at him, and he firmly grasped Alfonso's shoulder.

This was no dream.

"Would you like to see your father and mother?"

Alfonso nodded.

"What will you give me to see them?"

He looked down at the gold signet ring on his left little finger. His mother, Doña Luisa, had given it to him on his fifteenth name day. "This ring," he said to the guard, and with difficulty he removed it from his finger and handed it to the guard. The latter scrutinized it as if doubting its value, then finally nodded his acceptance.

"Come," said the guard. He pulled Alfonso to his feet. The guard stank of wine and garlic. Alfonso followed him to the door, which the guard opened. The little round man walked with an unsteady gait, holding a wineskin from which he drank in deep gulps.

When they reached the patio, Alfonso saw that it was night. Above them shone stars, and a faint sliver of new moon. It was deserted. Evidently everyone was asleep.

The guard offered Alfonso a drink from his wineskin. He took a swallow.

The guard led him along empty corridors and down flights of servants' stairs until they reached an underground passageway. Their boots sounded against the stone flooring. The guard held Alfonso's right arm with one hand, while in the other he held a resin torch. He stumbled so badly that Alfonso feared he would fall, dragging Alfonso with him and setting them both aflame.

At last, the guard unbolted a thick wooden door and pushed it open. They entered a dark cell with an overpowering stench. When Alfonso stepped forward, he hit his head against the stone ceiling, and he had to crouch slightly.

The guard's torch lit up the figure of a man lying beneath a blanket in dirty straw. When the flame came close to the prisoner's face, he stirred and opened his eyes.

"Father!" Alfonso cried.

With his right arm, Don Carlos slowly raised himself up to a sitting position. His other arm dangled loose in its socket. His face contorted in anguish at the sight of his son. "Alfonso! I thought you were off at sea."

"I came back."

Tears glittered on his father's sunken cheeks and trickled into his beard, which had turned entirely gray. "Evil days have fallen upon us! Oh my son, may God protect you."

Alfonso put his arms around Don Carlos. His powerful father, who once seemed like a giant, now was frail and old. When he looked down at his father's right hand, he saw that a fingernail had been torn out. Puss oozed from the wound.

"What have they done to you?"

"They stretched me with cords. They stretched this arm out of its socket," he said, rubbing the one that hung uselessly. "But I know nothing," he said, fixing Alfonso with a burning gaze. " I know no one. I know nothing." He glanced up at the guard, who was swaying on his feet from the effects of the wine. "I know *no one*," he repeated. Then he leaned forward and whispered into his son's ear, "I will die in the Law of Moses. . . . Alfonso, I pray for a miracle to save you." Don Carlos embraced him.

By now the guard could barely stand, for he had been drinking continually from his wineskin. Wobbling, holding the wall for support, he handed the torch to Alfonso.

He led Alfonso to Doña Luisa, who was seated on a low stool, staring straight ahead at the wall as if bewitched. Her cell, like that of Don Carlos, was low-ceilinged, and reeked of human waste. A narrow upper window let in a bit of light.

When Alfonso looked into her face, she did not recognize him at first. Her eyes had lost all luster.

And Alfonso knew in that instant that she had broken.

With a tremor of fear, he wondered whom she had betrayed.
"I'm your son!" he cried. "Alfonso, your son!"

She stared at him vacantly.

"Oh Mother!" He shook her shoulders. "Luisa! Maruca!
he cried, calling her by her pet name. It's me!"

She blinked her eyes then, and she seemed at last to realize who he was.

Her hair, long and white, fell in ragged tresses over the
flimsy rags she wore. Her feet were bare, covered with scabs.

"I am queen of rats," she murmured.

Shedding all modesty, she tore open her rags to show him
thick raw scars from beatings across her right breast and
stomach. Alfonso lowered his gaze.

"Look!" she cried, raising his face with her hand. "Look
what they did to me!"

"My poor Mamá." Gently he covered her breasts with the
ragged cloth.

"Oh Alfonso, I loved you the most!" Sobbing, she clung to
him as if she were a child.

He caressed her bony back and shoulders. "Mother, I
love you. May angels be with you."

"Help me die!" Her face was drawn with pain.

"Come on, you son-of-a-bitch!" cried the guard, giving
Alfonso a kick. "If I don't get you back, we'll both be in trouble."

Murderous rage surged up in Alfonso. He could easily
strangle the guard, set his hair on fire with the resin torch. But
what then?

"Not yet," murmured a voice inside him. "Not yet."

When the guard stumbled in the dark corridor, Alfonso
steadied him by the elbow and gently took the torch from him,
lighting their way.

*May you survive! May a miracle protect you. May angels
watch over you.* Alfonso could feel his father's and mother's
prayers for his survival. But how could he live if the
Inquisitors crippled him as they had his father?

God help me, he prayed. Guide me. If you want me to
live, show me the way. If you want me to die, let me die uphold-
ing Your Law, God of Israel.

He thought of Aunt Silva, who could sing like an angel.
Where was she? She had foreseen all this in the nightmares
that tormented her.

"Where is my aunt?" he asked.

"A small, white-haired woman? They say she died of
fright before the Holy Cross," said the guard. "They say she
was a witch."

Poor frail fluttering woman like a moth. She had no
witchcraft in her, save that of music and dance.

In silence, broken only by the guard's heaving breaths,
they made their way back upstairs to Alfonso's room.

After Matins had sounded the next morning, just as
Alfonso was squatting over the chamber pot, the round-faced
guard accompanied by a thin, sallow-faced companion entered
his room. Hastily he stood up. They let him fasten his breeches, then chained his wrists together and led him into a narrow
room, nearly bare of furniture, where three Inquisitors and a
scribe, all in black, sat at a table.

"Alfonso Valdez, have you at any time followed the Law of
Moses?"

What should he say? What his mother told them? What
had others confessed. Why did they bother to question him at
all? He tightened his sphincter muscles, holding back the need
to shit. He hadn't had time to do so before they took him here.

"Well, speak up."

I said nothing, Alfonso. I knew nothing. His father's
whispered words echoed inside him.

"Señores, I know nothing about this law."

The Chief Inquisitor flushed with anger. "Don't play the
innocent!" He had pale, parchment-like skin, a white goatee,
and a nervous way of scrunching up the left side of his face.

"I believe in Our Lord," said Alfonso, gazing at the ebony

crucifix on the wall for strength. The ebony carved Christ
seemed to change expression ever so slightly.

Their questions drummed into his brain.

"Is it true you bathe and change into clean linen on
Fridays?

"No," he declared.

"That you eat no pork?"

"No, Señores."

"Admit you scoff at the Blessed Virgin and at the
Immaculate Conception!"

"No, no!" he cried.

"Alfonso, have you at any time followed the Law of
Moses?"

"No. I have not."

"Admit you have spit out the Communion wafer in
secret."

"Admit you have eaten *matzas* that were made with the
blood of Christian children"

No . . . no . . . no . . . no, Señores . . . no.

"You're stubborn! Witnesses tell us otherwise!" cried the
Chief Inquisitor at last, his patience exhausted. He pulled his
black robes more tightly around him as he stood up. "Take
him into the sacred room, the *Camera Sancta.*"

They led him through an arched corridor into a windowless room with white walls, bare of any ornamentation save for
a raised altar at one end with a large wooden cross. Guards
stripped him to the waist and bound him to a vertical coffin-
like structure with movable planks to which they tied his arms.
One Inquisitor gave a slight turn to a wheel to which the ropes
were attached, and the planks beneath his arms moved out-
wards, stretching his arms painfully from their sockets.

"The Holy Church is merciful. But she routs out heretics.
The rack will stretch your joints until we hear the truth from
your lips. . . . Give us names of other Judaizers, and we'll
spare your parents. You have the power to spare them a great
deal of suffering."

It's too late for that, I fear.

"I don't know . . . I don' know. . . . I love the Lord Christ." he said over and over in response to their questions.

"Repent your sins. Confess your heresy. With whom did you attend Hebrew services? Give us names so that we may cleanse the soul of Spain."

He remained silent. The Chief Inquisitor gestured to one of the guards, who turned the wheel. The pain increased, as his arms were stretched almost to their breaking point. *Alfonso, I told them nothing.* In his mind the four letters of J-H-W-H glistened like white fire bright against surrounding blackness. He focused on the letters with all his might, in order to endure what might come.

"Give us names."

The wheel again turned, and he felt his arms about to burst out of their sockets. His mind went wild with fear. *They will cripple me.* Then he felt hot urine running down his thighs. Excrement hit his ankles, and a foul odor filled the air.

"Take this unholy *animal* away!" shouted the Chief Inquisitor.

A pewter basin with lemon-scented water. Fragrant Castile soap. Clean breeches and clean white linen shirt. But his blue leather vest . . . . before his voyage with Miguel . . . now it seemed a lifetime ago ... his mother had sewn gold pieces into its lining. Where was it? When he found the worn vest crumpled beneath the new breeches, he sighed with relief.

A key turned in the lock. A tall priest entered. He had a gaunt, ascetic face.

This priest also looked vaguely familiar from another time. Was it possible that the priest had attended the Seder service with the Duke of Cádiz long ago? The priest sat down on the edge of the bed. "You're a handsome lad," he said to Alfonso. "In case you're wondering, it was I who sent you the soap and water for washing. You Marranos do enjoy cleanliness." The priest's voice was too smooth, and when Alfonso

looked into his eyes, the priest glanced away. Alfonso did not
trust him. Probably this priest had been given the task of
obtaining information from him by gentler, more insidious
methods.

The priest then led Alfonso outside to a patio, where a
servant brought them trays of delicacies: roasted squab, fresh
greens, honey pastries, and country wine, all of which Alfonso
devoured hungrily.

They watched the sun set beneath red tiled rooftops.

The priest talked of how he had been inspired through
prayer to take Holy Vows, and he spoke of having experienced
ecstatic visions. But Alfonso did not believe him. The priest's
voice was too unctuous. There were words, gestures, glances
that did not fit together.

"You too have suffered, I know. You've been torn
between the innocent faith of your childhood and the way of
your forefathers."

How did this priest know so much? Perhaps he had been
talking with Father Juan. Perhaps they had arrested him, too,
and had tortured him to obtain this information.

Alfonso was silent. He gazed at the bloody pink glare in
the sky left by the sunken sun.

Then the priest spoke again, fondling one of Alfonso's
knees as he did so. "I don't care what doubts you've suffered.
If you will let me love you, I can spare you further suffering."

Alfonso recoiled beneath his touch. The priest's long fingers felt cold and reptilian. His fingers crept up Alfonso's
thigh, lingered on the inside, crept towards his groin. Then he
drew back, as if he had touched a blazing coal. "You're handsome, Alfonso," he murmured. "Too handsome. Perhaps the
Devil has sent you to tempt me. Yes, it's the Devil in you," he
said, speaking more rapidly. "The Devil draws my hands to
your flesh and incites impure thoughts."

"Señor, I have no desire to tempt you in any way."

"It would be a pity to maim your body," the priest said
softly. Then more abruptly, "Do you find it in your heart to

repent of your sins and confess to the Mother Church?"

"Confess what?"

"Duplicity."

Blood rushed to Alfonso's face, and he broke out in a sweat.

"The Holy Church is as zealous as a mother with her newborn babe. If we deal harshly with the body, it's to save the soul for eternity."

"You want to sport with me, as a man sports with a woman. Where does that fit into Church doctrines?" Alfonso looked directly into the priest's pale green eyes.

"The Devil has sent you to tempt me!" cried the priest. Then he stared past the patio wall, reflecting. "The Holy Scriptures say 'If thine eye be evil, pluck it out.' When I was a youth, I took monk's vows in order to lead a pure life. Then I hearkened to how Satan had crept into my spirit, despite my efforts. For years I have fasted, worn a hair shirt underneath my robes, and I scourged myself with whips."

Again his tone softened. "Alfonso, my lad, I'm fond of you. Repent your erroneous thoughts. Repent and embrace Our Savior." His hand brushed Alfonso's cheek as he leaned forward, his lips moving close to Alfonso's, as if to plant a kiss.

"Our Holy Savior was a Jew."

"Satan is in you!" cried the priest, losing all patience. He clapped his hands, and guards appeared out of the shadows. "Take him back to his room at once!" he cried.

His quarters became a dungeon cell, dark, small, stinking, lined with straw, like his parents' cells. Barefoot – they had taken his shoes – he stepped on dried excrement.

Were his parents still alive? He prayed for them. Half delirious, he thought he heard them moaning aloud. He vowed that should he ever escape, he would circumcise himself. He had heard of Jews who circumcised themselves in prison with knives or sharp stones. If he had a sharp instrument, he would do it now.

I told them nothing, Alfonso.

His mother had gone mad because she could not endure the physical pain.

Why, he wondered, hadn't his ancestors left Spain two hundred years ago when the persecutions began? But where would they have gone? Two hundred years ago Jews could no longer dwell in France, because people there believed they had caused the Black Death. His forebears could have fled to North Africa, Salonika, or other parts of the Eastern Mediterranean. But their roots in Spain had been too deep.

Father Juan had told him that each action is recorded for eternity in what Kabbalists call Akashic Records. No leaf falls, no creature draws a breath without leaving an invisible impression. His human life was only a flicker of time, of light in the world, while his bravery or cowardice would cast ripples forever.

Rats scampered across the stone floor. The stench was so strong he could scarcely breathe. But above him was a narrow, barred window. A tiny bit of light shone in. Blades of grass poked in between the bars.

"Where are your brothers?" they asked. "Where are your cousins?" He thanked God that both his brothers as well as Aunt Silvia's sons, Arturo and Diego, were in far off lands.

"Where is Emilia, the *conversa.*"

You can cripple me, but I will not tell.

He stared straight ahead at the ebony Christ and said, "I love the Lord Jesus with all my heart."

"If you truly love Christ, then give us names."

He said nothing.

The Inquisitors conferred in low voices, but that day they did not torture him further.

Day after day of questioning:

"Did your family light candles on Friday nights?"

"They did so every night, Señores."

"Did they light them in a special way on Friday, as Jews do on the eve of their Sabbath?"

"Señores, I don't know."

"Did they don clean clothes on Saturdays?"

"No more than on other days, Señores."

"Did they keep the Holy Days of Jews?"

"Señores, I don't know."

"Did they fast the fasts of the Jews? Did they eat unleavened bread? Did they pray the prayers of Jews.. Did they read Jewish books?"

"Señores . . . I don't know . . . I don't know . . . I don't remember."

"Did you follow the law of Moses while feigning to be Christian?"

Alfonso was silent. When he tried to speak, the words stuck inside his mouth. He felt paralyzed. Visions of himself burning at the stake passed through his mind.

If he said the words that he wanted to say, "As a Jew I live and as a Jew I die," then all would be lost, for he would be given into the hands of the State to be burned as penance for his past heresy.

As a Jew I live and as a Jew I die. Viva la ley de Moisés!

Strange were their procedures. They knew he was guilty of heresy. Yet they awaited his formal confession. They were willing to wait, to question him for days and weeks, even months, and to put him through torture in order to satisfy their twisted legal proprieties.

So he must play along with their mad logic. He must resist. *God help me. Jesus help me,* he silently prayed, gazing at the Christ carved out of ebony.

"Give us names of Judaizers who attended Hebrew services with you," they repeated. "Surely Emilia, the *conversa*, was among them."

But he said nothing.

Then they held him down on a stone bench and placed a

cloth over his mouth. A torrent of water flooded his throat.
They were drowning him. He held his breath, choked, swallowed, and the cloth sank down into his throat. He was dying.
He saw flashes of brilliant light. Orange, scarlet, green, and
bold. His chest and lungs were going to explode. Then they
drew the cloth out, along with bits of his own inner skin. He
coughed, spitting out water and blood.

"*Hombre del diablo*," muttered the round-faced guard.
"Your mother died last night"

His throat was raw and burning with pain. If he yelled
aloud here in his cell, would anyone hear? It hurt his throat to
make any sound at all. Hours later, half-asleep, he felt a rat
nibble at his ankle. He kicked it as hard as he could against the
wall. It pounced down on him. With a shout, Alfonso grabbed
and choked it, barely evading its sharp teeth. Then he trampled on it with his callused feet until it lay still, no longer heaving. But afterwards, he felt its puncture marks on his skin,
and he wiped away a trace of blood.

Thoughts create forms.

Forms create substance.

If one was harsh with the husk, peeling it away, the sweetness of the marrow would be revealed. "*Pain is only a garment which conceals God. Remove it, and call on Him for
help.*" Kabbalistic thoughts such as these helped sustain him.

"Forgive these men, as God forgives you. They know not
what they do, and they are tormented souls," whispered the
Jewish Christ, floating invisibly.

"How can I forgive?" asked Alfonso.

The question remained unanswered, and the Holy
Presence faded.

He must break his attachment to his mortal body. Only
the spirit lived eternally. He looked at his light brown skin, his
black hairs. Veins protruded on his hands. Beneath layers of
clothing lay his wrinkled scrotum and his penis, wilted except
at night when, despite the terror of his situation, at times he

awakened with it swollen, hot, and throbbing, the semen wanting to burst its confines. Sometimes he awakened with soaked breeches. The semen would dry stiffly, chafing his thighs.

A horse neighed. A dog barked. Emilia seemed to float over him in a white dress, like an angel, her black hair streaming around her.

Emilia merged into the *Shekhinah*, Hebrew angel of mercy. She stroked his brow, soothed his aches with balm, planted a full, soft kiss on his lips. In the darkness, he could hear what sounded like a rat gnawing amidst the straw. Sitting up, he tried to ascertain where the creature was. At first, he could see nothing in the darkness. But the gnawing ceased, and everything became very still. Then the room grew brighter, as if faintly lit by moonlight. But how could it shine in here underground?

He looked up at the bars on the window above him. *Try them*, said an inner voice. There were three iron bars, long and narrow. A faint light shone in. From the moon? Odd that the moon should cast this much light. The light intensified. *Ein Sof*, Kabbalists believe, the Limitless One is light. Pure light. *Ein Sof* emanates light through infinite worlds. If our faith were pure, they say we could possess the power of *Ein Sof*.

All became strangely calm. The light shining through the narrow window gleamed brighter. In that moment, he knew he was going to live. He would escape. *Ein Sof* would give him the power.

Try the bars. As he gazed at them, the stone which embedded them seemed to crumble ever so slightly. He pulled the right-hand one. It wrenched loose. Another hard pull, and the bottom mooring gave way. As if under a spell, he concentrated with all his strength on the left-hand one. It too wrenched loose. The middle one however, would not yet give.

He stared at it, not quite sure why he was doing so, yet knowing that he had to do so. Under his gaze, it was slowly crumbling. Solid stone was pulverizing, as if centuries of time had dissolved its strength.

Now, whispered the voice. *Pull!* Exerting all his strength, he pulled hard on that central bar, and then he felt it give suddenly, pitching him forward against the wall.

Invisible hands seemed to help him clamber up to the window ledge. He held onto the bars, which were still anchored in their upper moorings. The pain in his arm sockets flared. No matter. Soon he would be free. God help me. *Ein Sof*, fill me with Your power. Invisible hands held the bars fast for his support.

As if under a spell, strangely calm, he crawled through the narrow opening, falling head first into a filthy moat of water. Cold and wet, he emerged, stumbling onto his feet. His head was bruised, but otherwise he had not hurt himself. He shivered with cold. Where would he go now?

In front of him loomed a high wall. On the other side he heard a night watchman ringing his bell as he cried out, "Three o'clock. All is well."

Alfonso waited until he heard the night watchman's footsteps recede.

In the darkness, the moon cast shadowy light on a tree. Alfonso ran towards it, climbed one of its low-hanging branches, made his way to the top of the wall, and jumped down onto a bed of shrubbery.

Staying close to the walls of buildings, under their protective shadows, he limped, barefoot as he was, through the cobblestone streets towards Father Juan's dwelling near the old church. When he knocked at his door, he could hear the priest snore. Alfonso kept on knocking and knocking, until at last Father Juan awakened. "Who is it?" he called out.

"Alfonso."

Cautiously he opened the door a crack. When he recognized the youth, he pulled him inside and embraced him. "Alfonso!" he cried. "Thank God you're alive."

CHAPTER 12

At dawn they walked through the northern gate of the city. Alfonso wore a brown Augustine monk's robe, his hair covered by a woolen cap beneath the cowled hood. The boots that Father Juan had given him already hurt his feet. He ached all over and he felt as if he were still covered with filth, despite the hot water in which he had bathed. To quell the pain, he drank *aqua vitae* from the priest's flask.

"You're fortunate they didn't pull the bones out of your sockets," said Father Juan as they trudged along.

At this, Alfonso broke down. Sobbing as they made their way along the muddy road, he told how the Inquisitors had tortured his parents.

Rain began to fall.

At midday, chilled and wet, they reached a village where they purchased horses with one of the gold *reals* that Doña Luisa had sewn so carefully long ago in the lining of Alfonso's worn blue leather vest, and which by the grace of God he still possessed.

They rode through rain-soaked mountain passes towards Seville. Was Emilia still there in her convent, or had *familiares* seized her, too? Numb with shock, he could scarcely react to this thought. Beneath them flowed the flooding Guadalquivir. The rhythm of his mare's feet jolted him. Feverishly, he smoothed his hand along her brown neck, sleek with rain.

By the third day of their journey they were itching all over, especially in their private parts, because of tiny mites they had picked up in the large beds they shared with other travelers at wayside inns. Moreover, Alfonso's horse began limping from a stone in one of her forefeet, which they were not able to dislodge. For hours the poor creature stumbled along in the mud until they reached a village with a blacksmith, who removed it. He gave them balm to use on the horse's foot at night when they stabled her, and Alfonso also used it to good effect on his aching muscles.

Nightmares tormented him. He twitched, trembled, and moaned in his sleep. More than once he awakened choking, gasping for breath from a dream in which men were pouring water down his throat and he was drowning. The priest would draw the youth towards him, calming him with the heat of his own body. On Alfonso's other side, a stranger might lie sleeping.

The fourth day, they approached Seville. The rain had let up, and the sky was brilliantly clear. From afar gleamed the red tile roofs of the city, amidst which soared cathedral steeples and the minaret of a former Moorish mosque.

As they rode towards the Plaza Mayor, they heard tinkling lepers' bells. A crowd of beggars surrounded them. One thrust his face close; it was half-eaten away. At once the others tore open their rags to reveal white mottled patches of flesh on faces, throats, and other parts of their bodies.

Their leader reached out for Alfonso with claw-like hands. Fearful of contacting his deadly malady, Alfonso dug spurs into his weary mare and whipped her into a gallop. However, the priest quickly tossed coins into their midst, for which they began scrambling like hungry gulls.

The beggars' cries rang in their ears as they rode on.

They secured lodgings on the upper floor of a house near the Port. That night Alfonso could not sleep. Juan's snores were loud in his ears. And he was plagued by his memories, agitated and restless over what was to come as well as by the thought of Emilia.

It was unseasonably warm for February. The stars shone large and brilliant. Ships creaked against their anchors. Smells of the briny sea-river assailed him, along with a stench of garbage and urine.

His feet were hurting dreadfully in Father Juan's ill-fitting boots

Prostitutes passed by, skirts rustling, smelling of cheap strong perfumes. These *mujeres de la noche* walked arm in arm or leaned languidly against buildings, waiting to mingle with sailors. One called out to him. Another clutched his sleeve, but he brushed her off.

Maricón, she yelled, and her companions jeered as Alfonso strode on.

He found himself in front of a cathedral, hateful yet alluring. He entered, bowing and crossing himself with holy water from a marble basin. The stones sounded against his ill-fitting boots, echoed against the vaulted ceiling. Wax tapers cast flickering shadows over carved wooden saints He fell to his knees before a small altar of the Virgin.

Immersed in prayer, he heard a rustling noise. Swiftly he rose to his feet and turned, just as a man leapt towards him. He gave the attacker a resounding blow, and the man fell backwards, his cloak spreading out like dark wings, crying out in pain as his head hit the floor.

Shaken, Alfonso reached the street. It was foolhardy of him to wander like this at night, but he cared little now if he lived or died. The half-full moon had risen high in the sky. He wandered into a tavern, sat down at a small table to ease his feet, and ordered wine. A rough-looking crowd frequented this place. They looked like thieves, whores, and drunken roustabouts. His own monk's robes drew curious glances.

A young girl sat down across from him. Her long dark hair hung loose. She looked no older than Emilia, with the same dusky skin. But there was a hard set to her lips and jaw. She wore a black gown with red ribbons at the bodice. "May I share your table, Father?" Her tone was slightly mocking. She leaned closer, and her breasts fell into view beneath the low-cut gown.

"Yes," he said, nodding.

"What are you doing here? This is not the sort of place that monks frequent." She took a sip from her goblet. A few drops of wine spilled onto her bodice – like blood he thought.

"That's a tale too long for the telling."

"I see," she said. "You prefer not to speak of your past."

The tavern boy put a plate of olives and cheese in front of them. She took a bite of olive, spitting out the pit into her cupped palm, then sipped more of her wine.

I come here every night," she said. "Surely you realize what I do for a living. My father, who treated me cruelly, threw me out onto the street when I was still a child. The one who saved my life – perhaps you have heard of her – was Susannah *la Hermosa*.

Alfonso's chest tightened. All Spain had heard of Susannah, celebrated for her beauty, the only daughter of a prominent New Christian, Count Diego de Susa, who had plotted an uprising many years ago against the Archbishop of Seville. He planned to battle the Inquisitors and drive them from the city. Priests and other noblemen plotted with the Count. If he had succeeded, perhaps the Inquisition would not have spread through Spain. However, he unwisely confided his plans to Susannah. Her lover, Federico, wormed the secret out of her. But while Federico pretended to be a converso, he was actually in league with the Inquisition. They forced her to watch her father and her six tall handsome brothers burn at the stake. After that terrible *auto da fé*, one of her admirers hid her in a convent outside the city. But she had returned to live brazenly as a prostitute.

"She was so beautiful," said the girl, leaning very close, so that her breasts almost touched him. "Yet she was miserable. She never forgave herself for her foolish trust in Federico, and as a penance she gave her body to anyone at all – nobles, beggars, sailors, cripples – the uglier the better.

"May God have mercy on her soul," said Alfonso, speaking as a monk.

"Her mother died when she was seven, and her father,

Count Diego de Susa, never remarried. He loved her perhaps too much." The girl gazed at him significantly.

"I lived with her in a house not far from here. But no one lives there now. She died just before Advent from the malady that sailors bring from the New Indies. For a long time she had been ill. She demanded that her head be hung from a meat hook above the front door after she died. 'Let my miserable life be a warning to all,' she said. She refused to accept the last rites."

Alfonso swallowed. He could not bring himself to speak.

"I can tell you too have suffered. I think perhaps you are *one of us*," the girl added in a low voice, leaning so close that her breasts brushed against his arm.

"No, *Señorita*," said Alfonso, all too aware of what she meant and of the presence of others in this noisy place. "May God have pity on your soul. I will pray for you," he said coldly.

The tavern boy whispered something in the girl's ear. She glanced towards a group of men at a neighboring table. "I have to go now," she said. Fear filled her eyes, and she trembled slightly as she stood up. "May God protect you," he said.

Soon after the girl's departure, Alfonso, too, felt impelled to leave.

Some force led him towards Susannah's street. The boots were hurting his feet almost unbearably. Worlds within worlds. Mirrors within mirrors. When he felt compelled to stop, he knew this was THE STREET. He turned onto it and made his way past darkened houses with no signs of life. A cat hissed in the darkness. A ray of moonlight through clouds disclosed rotting garbage beneath him on the paving stones.

Pity, sighed a voice inside him.

La Calle de la Muerte.

Susannah's head, dried and shrunken, was swaying above a door, half on its hinges. Wind rose up, creating a funnel around him. Her tresses lengthened and wove together, like tentacles of seaweed.

Pity . . . pity, moaned the voice in the wind. *You are one of us.*

The most extreme sadness pierced through him, and he wanted to surrender to the wind, yet he knew he must keep on going or he would be trapped inside it forever.

Inside the funnel of wind was a strange blue-tinged light, and then shapes emerged, as the wind's force died down. Young girls hovered like birds in bright Moorish silk pants and jeweled transparent gauze blouses. They were reclining on cushions, laughing, smiling. They wore gold bracelets and earrings and necklaces. He heard the tinkling of voices and metal.

Seaweed hair impaled on a hook. The brothel was abandoned.

The street was abandoned. All the neighbors had fled. His boots echoed against the cobblestones.

The lights grew brighter. One of the girls beckoned to him.

The empty houses seemed to be breathing, to be watching him.

He kept on walking, walking.

When he stumbled over a beam, he caught his balance and kept on walking. He ignored the laughter, the murmur of voices, the sensation of arms clinging around him.

A cat leapt after a rat, caught it, and crunched the animal between its teeth.

He kept on walking, barely conscious of where he was going.

At length he found himself beyond that accursed street, standing by the cathedral he had entered earlier. But it seemed changed. He heard faint sobbing, and he remembered a story he had heard as a child. People said that the summer after the *auto da fé* in which Susannah's family perished, plague infested the city. But Marranos (all New Christians were now termed Marranos in Seville) were forbidden to take refuge in the country. Then hundreds of them arrayed in velvets and silks gathered together and made their way to this cathedral. They were insane with grief, with fear for their lives, and they wanted to atone for their sins. When they reached this holy place, the Bishop with his bodyguards stood before them, forbidding them to enter. He had locked its doors.

Their grief knew no bounds. They groveled, shrieked, wailed, tore their garments, and went wild with despair, for they had abandoned their Jewish faith, and now the Christian Church would not take them. As he looked up at the walls of the cathedral, barely visible in the darkness, he could feel their suffering.

Slowly, carefully, his feet hurting more with each step, he made his way back to their lodgings. When he awakened in the morning he felt heavy and stuporous, as if he had drunk a quantity of inferior wine.

CHAPTER 13

"Stay here," said Father Juan as they reined in their horses beneath a grove of olive trees. In the distance loomed the low-lying buildings of the Convent Santa Carmen, the same one in which Susannah had briefly sojourned.

Emilia was inside those walls. Father Juan thought it would be easier to obtain her release if he came alone. He led Alfonso's mare with him for Emilia to ride.

Alfonso, dressed in a new suit of clothes for which a tailor had fitted him, sat down beneath a tree with a thick trunk and soaring branches. Soon, God willing, he would see her again! He stretched his toes inside his new boots. God bless his mother for her prescience in sewing those gold *reales* inside his vest. Thank God for the luxury of boots that no longer chafed and pinched . . . for hot baths . . . for the potion of bitter herbs that had quelled the bothersome mites.

Afternoon None bells sounded. He grew anxious. What if she had died? What if she had been disfigured with pox? What if she no longer loved him. And what if Inquisitors had arrested her?

Scent of lavender. The tiny flowers hung in pale, fragrant bunches from the ceiling. Emilia was folding freshly laundered linens, placing a few dried blossoms in each, when a nun summoned her to the Reverend Mother's office.

What have I done wrong? What has happened? she wondered.

Emilia had stomach cramps from her period, and she was bleeding heavily. She worried that the blood would seep through the rags and through her brown novice robe.

Weak from fasting, she felt a little dizzy as she walked along the corridor. She had imposed this on herself in order to purge her spirit of something impure and dark that she did not understand.

There was no one in whom she could confide. Certainly she could not divulge any scraps of information to her confessor, a cold and unsympathetic priest.

For weeks now she had been praying alone in the chapel while others were enjoying the hour of recreation after Vespers. She had not played the guitar or sung, except in choir. From afar she would hear her friends' voices raised in song and laughter. Most of them were well-born and awaited marriage. Their high spirits only intensified her prayers for purity, for a respite from the longing and lust for Alfonso which engulfed her, and for the safety of those dear to her. It had been too long since they had written to her.

"Please let them be safe. Let them be well. Especially Alfonso," she would beg the austere carved Virgin at the altar of the little chapel.

Half-starved from her fasting, reality around her seemed to subtly shift. One day the Virgin moved her lips ever so slightly. Was this a holy miracle or a diabolic illusion? Emilia prayed for protection from the Devil's lure.

Narrow beds with white sheets.

Alfonso's arms around her. His lips on hers. The texture of his flesh in her dreams.

Gray cotton nightgowns. Shivering in the early morning cold, she would wait her turn in the courtyard to wash her face and hands with icy water from the well.

The regularity of the day's routine, ordered by the ringing of bells at hours of prayer, gave her succor.

When she saw Father Juan in the Mother Superior's office, she cried out his name and rushed to embrace him. He pulled back slightly, and from the look in his eyes she knew that something was terribly wrong.

He gripped her hands for a moment, then let her go.

"Emilia, my child, I've talked with the Reverend Mother, and I've come to take you home," said the priest. "Doña Luisa fell from her horse a fortnight ago and has suffered grievous injury. Don Carlos and his sons are off at sea. So she has sent me – as I'm her cousin and closest kin – to bring you back to her side. They fear she's dying."

Emilia gave a piercing cry and clutched at a chair to keep from falling. Her legs trembled beneath her.

"I find it strange she did not send a *dueña*," said the Reverend Mother, giving him a sharp look. She had a round rosy face, thin lips, and eyes that seemed to see into one's mind. Like Father Juan, she wore brown Augustinian vestments.

"There wasn't time. I rode here as quickly as I could."

"I've known him all my life. He gave me First Communion!" cried Emilia.

"Why does no letter come from Doña Luisa confirming your mission?"

"She's too ill to write."

"Oh, please – I must go to her." Emilia began sobbing, twisting her handkerchief as if she would strangle it. She could feel blood flow more heavily into her menstrual rags.

The Reverend Mother whispered something to the other nun, who immediately left the room. Father Juan felt highly uneasy. Suppose they refused to let Emilia go?

As for Emilia, she realized more clearly now that something terrible had happened that he could not talk about. "Oh I *must* go!" she cried. She clutched at the rosary around her neck to give her strength. How pale and thin she had grown, thought the priest. Although her hair was hidden by the stiff, cream colored headdress of a novice, this did not hide her beauty.

"There is more to this tale than you've divulged," said the Reverend Mother. "Frankly, I question your story." She looked him directly in the eyes. *Inquisition* hovered in the air, unspoken.

She paused, collecting her thoughts. "Emilia, my dear, you may pack your belongings. Don't linger to say goodbye to anyone. If you leave with the good Father, you must do so at once." She caressed the girl's cheek, then leaned forward and kissed her quickly on the lips. "God be with you," she murmured. "*Cuidado.*"

Béatriz was mopping the dormitory floor on her hands and knees when she found Emilia packing her things into a leather bag. Béatriz flung her arms around Emilia's legs. "Don't go! Don't go!" she shrieked and sobbed. "You're my only friend. I'm afraid for you!" Her sobs rang in Emilia's ears as, trembling, shaking all over, she stuffed her bag shut and ran from the room.

As soon as the gates clanked shut behind them, the priest spurred his horse to a gallop, and she followed astride, her robes fluttering. When she saw Alfonso, she quickly dismounted and flung herself into his arms, laughing and crying all at once.

Late that night, long after Compline bells had sounded, the priest married them in a chapel hidden within the depths of the cathedral. There were no witnesses, except for mice that scampered in the shadows cast by votive candles. Emilia wore her only gown, which was of black silk, along with a necklace of pearls that Doña Luisa had given her and her mother's garnet earrings. She was still bleeding heavily, and she felt sick. They had told her about the fate of Alfonso's family under the Inquisition, about his escape, and she sobbed uncontrollably throughout the evening.

"Why get married at all?" she sobbed.

"Because I love you, and you love me – or you used to."

"I still do," she murmured.

She insisted on getting married within the Church, having evidently separated the Inquisition and Christ within her mind. Her conflicts, in fact, were similar to what Alfonso's had been.

"*Deus vos beneficat, uomo et matrii*," chanted the priest. Then he added in Hebrew, "*Yevarekhekha*, May God bless you." From beneath his monk's robe he produced a goblet wrapped in a napkin, and he ordered Alfonso to smash it with his right foot. This he said was to commemorate the fall of the Temple in Jerusalem.

Emilia was perturbed by the introduction of Hebrew ceremony. It seemed a betrayal of the Church. She felt dizzy, close to fainting, and Alfonso had to hold her arm to steady her as they walked back to their lodgings. She felt wet with blood and needed more rags. Embarrassed, she whispered her situation to Alfonso.

That night the two of them slept in each other's arms, fully clothed, curled up in a corner on the floor, while Father Juan sprawled over the big bed.

In the morning they left the city in a newly purchased carriage. They were journeying to Lisbon, where people said it was easier for Jews to live. King Emmanuel of Portugal, repenting his past harshness – the forced baptisms of 1497 and the multitudes of children who had died afterwards on the barren island of Saint Tomás – had signed an edict granting all New Christians twenty years of immunity from the Inquisition.

Thinking it safer for Emilia to travel as a man, Father Juan had procured for her loose breeches, a man's shirt, and a cloak. She tied her long dark hair back beneath a loose-fitting chamois cap.

When she put the clothing on, for a little while her old gaiety returned. She laughed with pleasure. "It's so much more comfortable to dress this way! I shall do so from now on! But I want my hair unbound!" She whirled around the room, humming a tune that Aunt Silvia had taught her long ago.

But then her grief welled up again, and she wept as they left Seville behind them. She wept over what the Inquisition had done to all of them. Clutching her prayer beads as well as

the silver amulet that her mother had given her, she prayed for
Silvia, for Luisa, for Carlos, that their souls might find peace.

They traveled westward past vineyards, olive trees, and
fields where laborers were sowing spring wheat. At a deserted
spot by a clear stream, they stopped to water their horses and
to refresh themselves.

"Eat, my child," Father Juan commanded Emilia. They
had stopped for the night at a wayside inn, crowded with
rough travelers. She was relieved to be in male clothing, and
she spoke scarcely a word, not wanting her voice to belie her
male disguise. The only women in evidence were the serving
maids, who laughed coquettishly at ribald remarks and lustful
squeezes on their buttocks and breasts and who seemed ready
to offer themselves for further pleasures.

She had eaten and drunk nothing all day save a few
morsels of bread and a few mouthfuls of water from the
stream. The greasy stew of meat and onions in the pot nause-
ated her. Alfonso, seeing this, went into the kitchen and
secured a thin slice of rare venison, goat cheese, and dried
dates, along with a carafe of their best wine, secured by slip-
ping a coin into the cook's hand.

"Drink," he urged. "You must drink. Eat just a few
bites," he cajoled.

But she only nibbled at the food.

Later that night after Juan had gone to sleep in a big
featherbed in which lay three or four other travelers, Alfonso
and Emilia crept outside into the barn, where they found a
pile of soft hay. A bit of moonlight shone through an open window. He pulled her down and lay on top of her, and they held
each other as tightly as they could. When he tried to remove
her clothing, she resisted, because she said she was still bleeding.

He kissed her passionately, sticking his tongue deep into
her mouth, while his hands squeezed her buttocks. "Please,"
he implored.

Finally she let him remove her upper garments and let

him gaze on her body. He suckled at her nipples, while she ran her fingers through his hair.

Then they heard a rustling sound. Footsteps. Someone clearing his throat. Spitting. Hastily they dressed – for he had slipped down his breeches – and lay still. The man trampled through the hay, then lay down only a few paces distant from them . Soon he began to snore.

Alfonso was aching with lust. Quietly he opened his breeches and guided her fingers around him and thrust against her until his liquid spurted out onto her hand and clothing. If only the blood would stop.

In the morning Alfonso brought her a guitar he found at the market. She would play and sing as they drove along the road, her hair swinging loose when the three of them were alone.

She began to eat again, a few mouthfuls at first, and then more. Alfonso searched for foods that she might savor – figs, oranges, almonds, pomegranate juice preserved with wine, olives, fresh-baked pastries, fish from mountain streams which they could bake over fire.

They traveled through forests and after a few days ascended into the mountains, where villages were small and far apart.

Some nights they bedded in the open air under brilliant stars, hearing occasional owls hooting, rustlings of night creatures. Father Juan arranged to leave the young couple alone frequently, shouldering more than his share of the daily tasks. He wanted them to take joy in each other while they could. What lay ahead in the future gave him cause for fear.

To her despair, she kept on bleeding. Perhaps she was cursed like the woman in the Bible whom Christ healed by his touch. Alfonso and Father Juan insisted that she drink wine and eat red meat, but this had not helped.

She strummed the guitar for hours, whether singing or not, and the music lifted their spirits. She sang the songs Aunt Silvia had taught her long ago. She sang songs she had learned

in the convent from other girls, as well as songs she had heard
from wandering gypsies. Sometimes Alfonso and the priest
joined in.

> *I am a rose. I am a flower*
> *I grow in foliage where no sun has shone.*
> *Your sweet lips are a fountain of dreams*
> *My guardian angel has never drunk.*

Sometimes at night when she and Alfonso held each other
close, while she was drifting off to sleep Emilia seemed to hear
her mother crying out to her. *I will die soon because she wants
me with her*, she thought. But she didn't speak of this to
Alfonso.

The pleasures of their lovemaking, incomplete as it was,
put into sharper focus their grief for those close to them who
had suffered so much.

As for his brothers, Miguel and Rafael, were they safe?
And what about their uncle Rodrigo, his mother's brother who
had sailed off long ago with Cristóbal Colón and later settled
in Constantinople? Was he still alive? Perhaps they should
have gone to Rodrigo and sought his help.

Grief alternated with a kind of giddy lightness. One night
Alfonso and Emilia lay wedged between three travelers on a
broad featherbed, as it was raining too hard to venture outside. Alfonso drew her close and fondled her beneath the bedclothes. Then in a whisper she described how she and Beatriz
used to practice caressing and kissing in their convent bed at
night, as if one of them were a man. "Like this!" She giggled,
and blew into his ear. ·

In the morning other travelers talked of forming a little
caravan as protection against the brigands who frequented the
isolated mountain passes that lay ahead. "No!" said Alfonso
vehemently when Father Juan talked of joining the others.
"We're safer alone. If we were with them, Emilia couldn't sing,
for then they'd know she's a woman."

Emilia, clutching his arm, murmured her agreement.

And so they traveled on alone.

Fields gave way to parched earth, shrubs, sparse cypresses as they ascended the mountains. There were only a few villages far apart, small, impoverished settlements where people eked out meager livelihoods with a few sheep and a few crops that would grow in the arid, rocky soil – onions, a little wheat, olives, apples, spring greens. The road grew steep and narrow. Their horses needed to travel more slowly so as not to lose their footing and plunge off cliffs.

One morning Alfonso awakened with a strange feeling. Emilia's hair wound around him, mixed with wisps of hay. They were behind a barn. He knew something would happen – something ominous pervaded the atmosphere.

Their horses were tired, and the carriage was heavy for them to pull up the steep slopes. Father Juan suggested trading their carriage for another horse at the earliest opportunity.

Then late in the afternoon as the sun was beginning to set, it happened. Suddenly three men on horseback blocked their path.

Emilia, who had unbound her hair, had been singing one of Aunt Silvia's old melodies as they jolted along.

One of the riders grabbed the reins of their carriage horses. Another flashed a sword in Alfonso's face – he was in front driving. The third shouted, "A girl! A girl dressed like a man!" and tried to pull Emilia out of the carriage.

Then things happened so fast that afterwards they were not sure how or when things happened.

Alfonso drew his sword and slashed at the brigand who had pulled Emilia out of the carriage and who had hurled himself on top of her on the ground. She was screaming and struggling to get free.

The sword flashed through the air, barely missing her, thrusting deep into the brigand's left side. He roared with pain and collapsed on top of Emilia. Alfonso was just pulling her

out from underneath when he heard the priest cry out for
help. Emilia wriggled free, while Alfonso rushed to the priest.

The two other brigands fled on their horses.

Father Juan was lying on the ground in a twisted position.
He groaned when Alfonso tried to raise him up. His hip and
thigh had been injured.

"They took our purse," the priest murmured. He was
lying on his back. "I can't move."

Emilia and Alfonso helped him into a sitting position and
lifted him into the carriage, putting him in back so he could lie
down against the cushions.

"Sing to me, Emilia," he murmured. "It helps me forget
my pain.

Meanwhile Alfonso urged the horses on. It was growing
dark. They would need to camp out in the open that night.

While Emilia and the priest rested, he kept guard, barely
dozing off. In the distance a wolf howled. The priest was in too
much pain to sleep.

Alfonso had given what remained of his gold *reales* to the
priest, and they were in the purse which the brigands had
stolen. Now they had barely enough coins with which to feed
themselves and their horses on the rest of the journey – only a
few silver pieces which Alfonso had kept in his pocket.

At a marketplace, Emilia sold her gold brooch for one
hundred *dineros*, far less than its worth.

They slept in the fields or under trees. As they descended
the steep mountain slopes, it grew hotter and the sun burned
them by day.

When they finally approached Lisbon with its blue waters
and steep hills, there was not a breath of wind and the leaves
of trees were motionless. As they drove along its cobblestone
streets, an inexplicable feeling of dread seized Alfonso. He felt
a sense of doom beneath the white hot sun, the sparkling sea-
port, and the whitewashed buildings.

CHAPTER 14

The first few nights they slept in a church courtyard along with beggars, as they had no coins for lodgings. A merciful physician named Avram attended Father Juan, who was in constant pain. Through Avram, they learned of the Monastery of the Augustines, five leagues to the north. The physician let it be known that it was a refuge for monks of ambiguous persuasion where Father Juan might freely pursue his Hebrew studies. There, too, he would receive the care he needed while recovering from his injuries. The physician arranged to drive him there.

With sadness, Emilia and Alfonso bade the priest farewell.

A few years earlier Alfonso's cousin, Arturo, had settled in Lisbon and established his own shipping company. Now Alfonso inquired after him and found his office by the Port.

Arturo generously gave the couple money and helped them find lodgings. Heavier than ever, his round, good-natured face usually gleamed with sweat. He offered Alfonso a livelihood as his accountant.

While Alfonso and Emilia were moving in their meager household goods, a swallow, perhaps blinded momentarily by dust, flew headlong against the building and fell upon the cobblestones, its skull smashed by the impact. Emilia gave a little cry. "A bad omen," she whispered.

Finally Emilia's bleeding stopped, and they made love. It was on a Sabbath evening. Emilia had lit candles, covering her eyes with one hand as she murmured the Hebrew prayer she had learned from Arturo's wife. Here in Lisbon, by royal decree, they were safe from prying neighbors and safe from the Inquisition.

This was the first time that Emilia allowed Alfonso to see
her entirely naked, and they both gazed on each other in the
candlelight with a kind of awe. When he first penetrated her,
she cried out in pain, then bit down hard on his shoulder.
Afterwards they fell asleep entwined in each other.

Later on he awakened to find her running her hands over
the scars on his back. "The Inquisitors did *this* to you in
prison," she said, as she kissed the scars. You've never told me
exactly what they did to you. I want to know."

"I don't want to," he said.

"You *must*," she murmured into his ear.

"What happened will always haunt me."

"I know," she said. "Tell me about it. That will help."

In a whisper, as if afraid even now of a hidden listener, he
recounted fully what he had endured. He wept in her arms, at
last allowing himself to feel what he had compressed so tightly
within himself.

In the following weeks, she grew lustful. Her inner muscles would squeeze against him, her back would arch, and she
would rise against him, moaning with pleasure. The
Shekhinah, ancient Hebrew Goddess of Love, seemed to sur-
round them in a golden cloud. Sometimes Alfonso sensed light
enveloping them both, lifting them above themselves. For an
instant a veil would lift, and he would feel almost in union with
God.

Almost but not quite.

Understanding lay just beyond reach, tantalizing as a
mirage.

But then the veil would descend thick and dark. The
ghosts of those who had suffered and died crept into their
souls, and pleasure would be followed by waves of grief.

They lived above a grocery store in the New Christian
quarter or *alfama*. Their lodgings consisted of two rooms with
a balcony that overlooked a street so narrow one could stretch
out one's arm and almost touch the opposite building. Emilia

grew potted geraniums, thyme, lavender, yarrow, jasmine.
Their laundry billowed in the wind. If they looked out from
the balcony above the rooftops, they could see the rim of ocean
far out beyond the port, where water merged into sky. This
was as it had been in their childhoods, when they could look
out from the parapets of the big house in Cádiz, out beyond
the church steeple and red-tiled roofs to the sea.

Emilia's long black hair would wind around Alfonso,
binding him to her in their sleep. At times she slept with one
arm flung over her head, as if she were protecting herself.
They grew playful. She would laugh with delight when he
kissed her toes. He loved her feet, with their high, shapely
arches. When morning sunlight streamed in through the window, it framed her in gold.

She became pregnant, and this filled them both with joy.
He would caress her rounded, growing belly and speak to the
child inside, as if it could understand. They both believed it
was a boy.

She played the guitar Alfonso had bought for her on their
journey to Portugal. The instrument gave her great comfort.
Sometimes he played, too, and they sang the Andalusian songs
they had grown up with. Sometimes she played Portuguese
songs she heard on the street or from the musicians who
played at the outdoor market.

He resumed his study of *Kabbala* and *Talmud*. Father
Juan had grown old and frail quite rapidly, as though he had
spent his reserves of strength on their perilous journey. His
hip had not healed properly, and it was difficult for him to
walk. Then, too, the monastery was a half-day's journey.

Many New Christians wanted to renew their ties with
Judaism as well as to study the esoteric *Kabbala*, which
offered the glitter of a magical reality beyond the realm of the
senses. Avram the physician led a small study group, and
Alfonso began to work with him.

Avram was an intense man with a sharp-featured face, a
pointed chin, and blazing dark eyes. He believed in palmistry,

astrology, and in reincarnation. He promoted the Kabbalistic belief that the pleasures of lovemaking could lead to enlightenment. "As above, so below." he would say. "There is a mystical ether or subtle body surrounding the material flesh," he told his followers.

In their meditations they visualized flaming Hebrew letters, each of which corresponded to a number, also imagined as a flame. They sang, chanted, swayed back and forth as they prayed, and sometimes they danced in slow, measured steps, gradually speeding up, twirling as they held a Torah aloft.

These meditations usually took place in a windowless room in Avram's house. Alfonso would return from them in an exalted state of mind. His own dwelling would seem humdrum, and Emilia now appeared to him as hopelessly weighed down in a gross material world. He wanted her to share his exaltation. He even asked Avram if he could bring her. But Avram shook his head and vehemently said that no women were allowed.

He tried to teach Emilia their songs and their meditations. But outside of Avram's group, these practices lost much of their power. Their lovemaking was no longer blissful, as it had once been. He grew critical of her, noticing now her minor blemishes.

It was woman's role, said Avram, to awaken man's desire, which could lead to enlightenment. In dulling his desire, she was binding him in darkness.

Things changed after All Saints' Eve when Emilia gave birth to Carlito. For a while they were both filled with joy over their infant son. She would rock Carlito in her arms and sing to him. Her voice had a new sweetness, a new purity, he thought. Her face shone with an ethereal light as she gazed at the baby nursing at her nipple, her soft dark hair cascading over her shoulders. How full her breasts were now, with blue veins underneath the olive skin. She wore a sea green skirt and a white blouse of fine, soft material.

Street sounds wafted up through their windows. Women's

voices squabbling, vendors crying out their wares. Their rooms were filled with cooking odors of dried fish, thyme, garlic.

At night after the baby had fallen asleep in his cradle, they made love with renewed tenderness. They felt joined in body, in spirit. This was perhaps the happiest period of their lives.

The days grew shorter. An unseasonably cold wind blew on the night of *Rosh Hashanah*. As they walked towards Arturo's house to attend his dinner, Emilia felt a sense of dread. Carlito felt so warm against her, wrapped in his little cream-colored blanket of soft wool. She had not wanted to bring him, but Arturo's wife, Dorinda, had urged her to do so, as her relatives had not yet seen him. Now she wished she'd left him at home with the little girl downstairs to tend him and a cup of warm goat's milk to be fed him in tiny spoonfuls, when he thirsted.

A servant ushered them into the dining room, where the other guests had already gathered. In addition to Arturo and his wife, Dorinda, both plump and richly arrayed in brocade and satin, there were two other women, a man who walked with a limp, and a sickly, fair-haired little girl of about three.

As they entered, one of the women gave Emilia a glance that caused her to tremble and to tighten her grip on Carlito. When she looked at the other child, she saw that the little girl's eyes did not focus, and they were coated with a milky substance. Emilia realized then that she was blind.

Servants put savory dishes before them – partridges, venison, ripe fruits, almonds, and red wine. The table gleamed with white linen, silver plates, and there were precious goblets of Venetian glass. Arturo presided over the richly laden table, carving the roasted meat.

Carlito was unusually fretful all during dinner. And so Emilia retired to a heap of cushions in a corner of the room to nurse him, while Arturo said a Hebrew blessing. Then in

accordance with custom they ate apples dipped in honey so
that the coming year would be sweet.

The absence of older children at the gathering disturbed
Emilia, especially since Fabio, Dorinda's brother, and his
wife, Consuelo (the one whose initial glance had caused her to
feel so afraid) were both middle-aged. She remembered terrible tales she had heard about how Jewish children had been
taken away from their families.

"No honey can remove our bitterness," said Consuelo
now, as the others ate. She seemed to be responding to Emilia's
unspoken questions.

"It has been over four years since they took our children
from us," she said, glancing once again at Emilia with blazing,
hate-filled eyes. The air rippled, as if ghosts of these vanished
children had entered the room.

"You don't know what it is to have your heart's blood –
your children – torn from your arms. You Spaniards *got* by as
Marranos – swine is what you are indeed! But we did not pose
as Christians, and as a result our children perished."

"Enough!" cried Fabio, seizing her arm. Arturo's wife
began to sob, as did the mother of the little blind girl.

But after a moment Consuelo once again began to speak,
repeating the tale she had told so many times.

"They tore our three sons and our daughter from us by
force. They broke Fabio's leg because he was trying to protect
our children. That's why he limps now.

"I don't know whether Christians adopted our children
or if they died on the island of Saint Tomás, where most of
them were taken. Surely you have heard of that wretched hot
desert wilderness. The children, all newly baptized, were
abandoned there to die of hunger and thirst and illness."

Fabio spoke up. "Emmanuel ibn Ezra smothered his son
rather than have him baptized. Then he killed himself so he
and his son could die in the Law of Moses. Many other Jews
did the same."

Emilia gazed at them in sadness and shock. *The other*

*women were jealous of her healthy baby boy. Oh Carlito, my
lovely child. May God protect you.*

"Arturo and Dorinda are lucky because they never had
children. As for Claudia, she wasn't yet a mother," said
Consuelo.

"They locked hundreds of us in a courtyard for days. We
had no food. No water. They had gathered us there under the
pretext of giving us passes to board ships and leave Portugal.

"Then they dragged us by our feet or hair – any part of
our body – to a baptismal font. Some Jews already bereft of
their children cut their own throats rather than submit. We
are truly *anusim*, forced ones.

"You don't know suffering until you have lost a child,"
she said, looking sharply at Emilia.

"Calm yourself, Consuelo! ... Please excuse my wife. She
has suffered too much," said Fabio, putting his arm around
her. He had a sad, compassionate face.

Soon afterwards Alfonso and Emilia left. A light rain had
begun falling. Emilia shivered with cold and fear as they
walked back in silence to their lodgings.

Three days later Carlito fell sick. His ears became red
and swollen, and he ran a high fever.

"Consuelo has put the evil eye on him," said Emilia.

He had just begun to crawl. Only six months old, Carlito
had thick black hair and a lusty cry. They thought they perceived something of his grandfather, Don Carlos, in the fierce
determined way he would make his way across the floor, half
crawling and half paddling on his belly. Watching his strug-
gles, they would smile with tenderness and delight. Alfonso
would swing him to and fro by his hands to strengthen his arm
muscles. The baby liked this exercise, and he would cry out
with joy whenever Alfonso began this favorite game.

But now he was too sick to crawl or swing by his hands.
He lay hot and comatose in his cradle, barely moving when
Emilia smoothed his hair. She placed her mother's silver
amulet beneath his little pillow.

They called in Avram, who prescribed a cold bath and who mixed herbal potions. When he gently inspected the infant's ears, Carlito howled with pain and tried to cover them up with his tiny hands.

"If he does not pull through," Avram said, "you may take comfort in the realization that he will be reborn in a new body. The human spirit doesn't die. It reincarnates through thousands, even millions of lifetimes."

But this was of no comfort to Emilia. That night she rocked Carlito in her arms and sang to him until it was nearly dawn. When at last he fell asleep, she prayed over him in his cradle. "Jesus is the true savior," she murmured. "Our child is dying because we abandoned Christ."

All the next day she paced back and forth saying her rosary beads. "Hail Mary full of grace. The Lord is with thee. Blessed art thou among women and blessed is the fruit of thy womb. Oh Holy Mother, heal my child."

Carlito howled at the top of his lungs.

In desperation, they called in a healer or *ensalmador*, a man with hunched shoulders and a wintry gray hue.

He bent over Carlito, his slender hands on the poor, fevered little body, and pressed his lips against the infant's open mouth in an effort to breathe new life into him. Long ago Emilia had been saved by such a man, but this *ensalmador* was powerless to save Carlito.

After he left, Emilia kept breathing into Carlito's mouth as she had watched the healer do, until Alfonso finally pulled her away. "Let him sleep, *mi amor*."

In the morning Carlito was dead.

They buried him in a cemetery reserved for New Christians. Alfonso ordered a stone headstone carved with angels for his grave.

Afterwards they remained at home in mourning. But when Arturo and Dorinda, Joao and Consuelo came bearing food and condolences, Emilia shrieked at them to leave.

"Jewish devils!" she cried. She brandished the antique

silver cross that she had resumed wearing. "I spit on all of you. It is because we were false to the Church that Carlito died. May Jesus and Mary have mercy on his soul."

Teresa, the grocer's wife who lived below them, also a New Christian, crossed herself.

A flicker of something like satisfaction crossed Consuelo's face. Observing this, Emilia leapt forward and clawed Consuelo's cheeks so that the blood ran. Consuelo cried out with pain.

The other women pulled Emilia back, while she struggled and shrieked, cursing and spitting at them.

"Leave us be!" ordered Alfonso. "She needs to be alone." He, too, felt they were somehow the cause of Carlito's death. Perhaps it was exposure to chill and rain after the Rosh Hashanah dinner, although afterwards Emilia had warmed the infant by the fire. If only they had never gone to that cursed dinner!

"They poisoned him with their envy!" cried Emilia.

Long after the others left, she kept on screaming, crying, crazed with grief. She tore the curtains from their hangings. She hurled their crockery on the floor, smashing plates and cups.

Alfonso held her close. "Be quiet, my love," he said in a hoarse voice, while she struggled vainly to free herself from his grip.

Finally her cries died down, and he persuaded her to drink a sleeping potion that Avram had left with them. "God willing, we will have more children," he said. "Rest now. Lie down and rest."

"No child can ever replace Carlito."

In the days that followed, Emilia ate practically nothing at all. Nor did she wash herself. Her hair was a wild tangle. She stared vacantly in front of her. She slept huddled beneath a heap of shawls on the tile floor.

She talked disjointedly, mingling past and present – Carlito's favorite red rattle, the scent of jasmine blossoms long ago in Cádiz. She prayed to Jesus and the Blessed Virgin as well as to other saints, clutching her rosary tightly around her wrist.

In vain he tried to get her to eat. He stroked and comforted her on the rare times she would let him touch her.

Then one morning she was gone. Perhaps she had ventured to the market, he thought. Or gone out for a breath of fresh air at last. And for the first time since the funeral, he went back to work in Arturo's offices. All morning he tried to concentrate on the black numbers in the ledgers, biting one end of his dull quill pen.

When church bells sounded Sext at midday, he walked home, hoping to find Emilia there. Perhaps she had come to her senses, combed her hair, groomed herself, prepared a meal. But their rooms were empty. He nibbled at a slice of raw onion, stale bread, and a few olives, but he had no appetite for more.

All afternoon he searched for her, walking through the *alfama* and then along unfamiliar streets up a steep hillside, until he was high above the city.

When he came to a small blue wooden church, something impelled him to go inside, and there he found her stretched out on the floor before the main altar. He gently touched her shoulder. She opened her eyes and looked at him with alarm.

A priest approached. "She is bewitched," he said.

"Grief has bewitched her," said Alfonso angrily. He lifted her up into his arms, carried her outside, and set her on her feet, where she balanced unsteadily. She had grown so thin. Slowly he guided her back, supporting her as they descended the steep streets.

They passed a carpenter's shop which had small altars on display for sale. As they came closer, they saw that the altars were of beautifully carved mahogany.

"I want one," she said.

And so he installed one in their lodging.

For a long time each day she prayed in front of it.

They had not made love since Carlito fell ill, and Emilia refused to resume their former relations because, she said, they were now of different faiths. "Jews tried to kill my mother and me. They killed Carlito."

"My father, a Jew, saved you. Christian Inquisitors tortured and killed my family."

"I'm so confused. I don't know what is true or what to believe," she wept. "I fear Jews, and I fear Christians, too."

Although she returned to their bed she would not let him touch her.

CHAPTER 15

April, 1502 - July, 1506

"Women are frivolous," said Avram when Alfonso came to him in despair. "So Maimonides believed. He wrote that one shouldn't waste one's strength on them or be drawn in by their seductions. They are childlike, and their wills are weak."

"Emilia is not frivolous or weak. She's heartbroken over the death of our son." *How lacking Avram is in his knowledge of the human heart. Far too long he has been a widower.*

Alfonso continued to study Kabbala on his own, as its doctrines helped heal the wounds caused by the conflict he continued to experience between Christianity and Judaism. The issues were far from resolved, and Emilia merely carried fragments of his own beliefs to an extreme.

Finally, he journeyed to Father Juan in his monastery, seeking advice and consolation. The good priest had grown frail. In the last several months he had visibly aged years. Alfonso feared that he had not many more days on earth.

"One cannot hurry a woman over her grief," said Father Juan. "Don't burden her with your desire. Even be aloof. Let her begin to crave you." He lay his warm hands over Alfonso, and the younger man felt the fullness of Juan's compassion.

Within the peaceful confines of the monastery, Father Juan and Alfonso spent hours over several short passages from Torah, as if in this way they could pierce its veil and discern the white fire that lay beneath the dancing black letters.

Although his income was meager, Alfonso hired a serving maid to take over most of Emilia's former tasks: cooking, cleaning, laundering, drawing water from the well. For hours

Emilia would sit by the window, looking out dreamily. She began to sing to herself, at first only occasional bits of melody, and then entire songs. One day she picked up her guitar, which she had not played since Carlito fell ill, and she sang a song that the baby had loved. It was a simple child's song. In the middle of it, she became overwhelmed with emotion, and began to sob, burying her face against the guitar.

That night he awakened to find her clinging to him with desperation. A rage-filled lust stirred in him. He pinned her down and pulled her nightdress up above her waist, parted her thighs, then thrust into her with pent-up desire, ignoring her sobs.

Afterwards she wandered around their rooms in a daze. "You forced me!" she sobbed. "Heathen pig!"

"Forgive me oh Mother of Christ, for I have sinned," she sobbed, as she knelt in her long white cotton nightdress before her little altar.

Overcome with rage, he pulled her up by her hair, and for the first time in his life he slapped her – a hard swift blow across the cheek. "You're my wife!" he raged. "You're as much a heathen as I am – we are both Jews. Do you hear! We are Jews! Carlito is dead. No prayers will ever bring him back." Feeling a cruel rage, he tore off her nightdress.

Naked, she kicked and pummeled his chest, then sank her teeth into his arm. He jerked free of her, and she collapsed on the floor, clutching her knees to her chest, tears streaming down her face. Then he knelt and held her in his arms.

"It does our poor baby no good to mourn him forever."

He carried her over to the bed. This time as he looked down into her eyes, they softened. She pulled him close, burying her face in his shoulder. When he penetrated her, she was wet and slippery, and they melted into each other. They made love several more times that night, dozing off in each other's arms. She became the aggressor, riding him, moaning when she climaxed. Night after night they made love, and at times all was golden, fluid, melting, as if the *Shekhinah* herself had

descended upon them. But at other times Emilia would draw
back afterwards, her eyes cold and hard. At these moments
Alfonso felt invaded by an all-pervading darkness and by the
grief of women over centuries mourning their dead children.

Four years passed. Emilia gained weight. Her once bird-
like body grew luxuriant. Her humor became calmer. But sadness settled into tiny lines around her mouth and shone in her
eyes, especially when she was alone.

She gave birth to two more children, María Inés, whom
they called Maruca was born in 1503. She was small and delicate like Emilia, but her hair was the color of bronze. Tomás
came into the world a year later He was a fat baby who lusted
for the nipple, who walked at only eight months, and who
climbed over everything. They tied a rope around his waist to
keep him from falling out the windows.

The children soothed her pain, and her passion found
expression in maternal love for them. She and Alfonso took
joy in their children, and when Alfonso came home from work
he would find her singing, dancing, playing games with them.

"My darling raven, *mi amor negrita*," he would call her.
They knew each other, so they thought, to the marrow of their
bones. But does anyone truly know another, or does one only
know the stalks, leaves, and flowers, while the roots remain
invisible? Alfonso would ponder this in his meditations.

During these years they stayed in their cramped lodgings
above the grocery store. Alfonso continued to work for his
cousin, Arturo, but supplemented his income by tutoring boys
in philosophy, mathematics, and languages. He also continued
to study *Kabbala* with Avram.

At this time several rabbis in the *alfama* openly led
Hebrew services in private homes as well as in a school for
boys. These were euphemistically described as New Christian
gatherings. Everyone knew the truth, but under the terms of
the King Emmanuel's twenty-year Edict, they were protected
against persecution.

These rabbis considered Avram to be a heretic, because the Kabbalistic beliefs he taught went against many orthodox Jewish laws.

This deeply upset Alfonso's teacher.

One night when he had gathered his students around him, he railed against them. "These rabbis are no better than priests. Narrow-minded, they seek to curb our knowledge," he said, leaning forward towards his little group from his cushion at the head of a low cedar wood table. "Rabbis as well as priests want to keep us ignorant. The Church forbids us to think for ourselves, while rabbis forbid us to study ancient philosophy. They ignore the fact that Maimonides himself based his works on those of Aristotle."

The air was still in the windowless room. Alfonso felt oppressed by Avram's intensity. Candle flames flickered from candelabra on the table and from sconces on the wall.

"Between rabbis and priests there's little difference," Avram went on. "They are equally ruled by their lust for power. They blindly obey laws without observing their spirit. Jesus railed against the Pharisees. But in these modern times, rabbis are no better than Pharisees. They forbid us to study *Kabbala* because they fear its light!" he cried in a piercing voice.

A tremor ran through Alfonso at the boldness of the physician's words. For far milder speech, men had suffered *herem*, or excommunication from the synagogue and had been tortured and burned alive. Candle flames gleamed, casting shadows on the other men's faces, so that they seemed half spirit, half flesh. The odor of camphor and myrh mingled with the scent of their bodies. Beneath his legs, the stone floor felt cool.

"Priests and rabbis alike follow the forms of religion. But these forms are rooted in fear and ignorance. The *Kabbala* pierces through veils to spirit," continued Avram. "In the *Zohar* is written:

'As wine must sit in a jar
so Torah must sit in this garment
so look only at what is under the garment
so all those words and all those stories –
they are garments.'

"Truth is our nectar," he concluded. "Truth is worth more than the most precious gems."

Through the group passed a collective shudder of fear caused by recollections of what standing up for truth had cost. Several had lost their children to the cruel Portuguese baptisms of 1497. Afterwards, one man's wife had gone mad with grief and had drowned herself in a well. Another man had lost his parents, brothers, and sisters when they fled Spain in 1492 and perished of starvation on the shores of North Africa. Then during the time of the forced baptisms, the Portuguese took away his three children, who were the lights of his life. He learned that they had been fortunate enough to be adopted by Christians in the north, but knew not whether they were still alive.

The youngest in the group, a tall skinny boy of fifteen, picked up a tambourine and began to play. They took slow steps at first, stamping their feet in time with the beat. Then the rhythm quickened. Avram went into the center and began to whirl around. On and on they all whirled. Alfonso, growing dizzy, paused and for an instant saw Avram's face with a new clarity. A certain blind self-satisfaction marked the man's face, and Alfonso realized then that he could never truly trust him.

Nonetheless, he let himself be carried away by the rhythm, the chanting, the incense, and the mood of the others until a kind of moody ecstasy came over him.

That winter it rained not at all, and the summer was unusually hot. Crops were ruined. Famine came to the land. The once plentiful market stalls were nearly bare. Some days

Alfonso's little family ate only sharp-tasting onions and dry bread and drank brackish water, which they boiled. He and Emilia gave their children the most generous portions. But she was pregnant, and she had grown so thin that he feared for the unborn child. So he persuaded her to eat more, giving her most of his own share.

In bed, Emilia murmured as she lay against him, "I am so afraid. I am afraid for our lives."

In truth, her fears were not without cause. Famine and drought brought pestilence. The rats grew bolder with hunger, scurrying through the streets in daylight. Each day the plague claimed more victims.

Processions of penitents began to march through the streets, led by friars who held aloft heavy crosses. There were increased murmurings against the Jews. People said the Jews had brought down curses on the rest of the population. Gangs of Christian youths roamed the streets. Tomás and Maruca were kept inside and grew fretful.

One day they awakened to see huge number of ravens circling over the *alfama*. There were perhaps more than a thousand dark birds, so thickly massed that they blotted out a large part of the sky. Avram said this was a portent of enormous change.

The grocer's wife, Teresa, who lived below went into a difficult labor. This woman, who shared Emilia's mixed religious sentiments, had become her best friend. Emilia insisted on staying with her and assisting the midwife. Two days later, she came back exhausted. "Teresa and the baby will live," she sighed with relief.

But Alfonso was perturbed because she looked so thin and tired. "If you fall sick, then what will become of us?

"I had to help her," said Emilia. "She was here with me when I was in labor with Tomás and Maruca." She sank down on the floor, hugging her knees. "Perhaps as your *Zohar* says, our days are arranged for us before we are even born. What will be is fated."

The grocer, in gratitude for Emilia's help, brought them a basket of lentils, wheat, wine, and precious figs and oranges which he had hoarded. They savored the food for many days.

But the plague was growing worse. Each morning wagons full of corpses, heralded by mourning bells, drove out to the cemeteries. People became afraid to go outside. Dominican priests railed against the New Christians, the false ones in their midst, whom they claimed had brought about famine and sickness. "*Conversos* have impoverished you," they told angry crowds. "They have tainted the purity of our hearts with their lies and their greed. They hold the best offices with the State. They have robbed us of gold through their cunning."

People muttered that the Jews had cast an evil spell over the land.

During Lent, Father Juan died of a wasting disease. The despair which he felt about the present situation, so similar to what he had lived through in Spain, no doubt hastened his end.

With his death, Alfonso lost his dearest friend. For although he had not seen the priest frequently of late, he felt closer to him than to any other man.

Late one afternoon during Holy Week, Alfonso wearily put down his quill and blotted the ink on the ledger. Earlier he had been down at the docks taking inventory of a ship's cargo, and now he was tallying up figures: fifteen rosewood boxes of Indian cinnabar, twelve boxes of cloves, fourteen of mace, six measures of pepper, seventy-five bales of Algiers flax, sixty-three bales of Egypt cotton.

Wearily, he hunched over the table with his palms over his eyes to rest them as numbers whirled in his mind. He heard the door creak open, and he heard footsteps. "Look who's here," said Arturo.

When he opened his eyes, he saw plump, disheveled Arturo standing next to his brother, Miguel. His brother had grown taller, more wiry. In that first instant Alfonso saw dark flames of rage around Miguel's body, despite his roguish smile.

His hair was cropped as closely as a priest's, and he wore brown velvet, his doublet embroidered with silver thread.

As the smile left Miguel's face, Alfonso perceived that his lips emanated a thin, cruel blue flame.

"What's the matter? Don't you recognize me?" said Miguel.

"I am overcome," said Alfonso.

He had seen Miguel only a few times since their ill-fated voyage. Miguel had managed not only to save his own skin but to salvage three of their father's ships from the Inquisition by renaming them, changing their exteriors, and adorning their bowsprits with sculpted depictions of saints. Over the years Miguel had maintained commercial dealings with Arturo as well as with his brother Rafael in Amsterdam.

With a feeling of dread, Alfonso rose and greeted his brother. For in his mind, Miguel's savage beating of the cabin boy was linked with the Inquisitor's arrest of their family.

Miguel now told them that he was carrying nineteen Jewish stowaways in the hold of his ship. He had brought the Jews out of Spain from the port of Algeciras, and he was bound for Flanders. But he had run out of food, and he had run out of money. He needed their help.

Arturo, who had given Miguel thousands of cruzeiros over the years, shook his head. "I can give only a little," he said. "Dominican monks have taken my gold for funeral wagons and for the Church."

Miguel then turned to his brother. "Come with me," he implored. "I'm going to Cintras to ask Count Manuel de Villanova for help. Your presence would help immensely, as I hear he's fond of philosophical discussion. That's something in which you are far more adept than me."

There are events that obey a mysterious and fatal rhythm. What if Miguel had not arrived like a ghost out of the past on the very day that he did? What if the Count had not asked the two brothers to linger another day? What if he had not allowed his own vanity to influence him? What if he had

simply refused to go? For years afterwards, Alfonso tormented himself with these questions.

But he had visited Miguel's ship at dusk, and the miserable conditions of the pale, starving stowaways so affected
him that he could not say no.

He awakened in fear, sweating and trembling. Emilia was
also awake, and she grabbed his hand. "You must go," she
whispered, as if reading his thoughts. "You must follow the
urging of your heart. While you're gone, I'll pack our belongings, so we 're ready to leave as soon as you return, my love."

Tenderly she held him close against her.

Miguel had shared their frugal fare of onions and bread
that evening, and he had urged them to sail with him to
Flanders, as Lisbon was now too dangerous. In Brussels or
Amsterdam, their lives would be easier, he said.

"What do you think we should do?" Emilia had asked
after Miguel had left. Alfonso had picked up a yellow onion on
the table in the kitchen and held it between his hands, then put
it to his face, sniffing its odor. It was nearly the only food they
had in the house. He was beyond hunger; there was simply a
constant dryness in his stomach. But when he gazed at her thin
face with its sunken cheeks; when he looked down at the children asleep on their pallets, both sucking on their thumbs as
if they were dreaming of food, he told Emilia to prepare herself and the children for the journey.

They would sail for Flanders with Miguel.

It was Good Friday when he and Miguel set out for
Cintres on horseback. That morning the sky had a pale green
glow. A flock of ravens had reappeared. They were circling
overhead, searching for prey.

Later he would reflect with a knife-sharp grief how all
things are connected, above and below. The tiniest action,
each breath one takes causes infinite ripples. What if he had
refused at the last moment to go, obeying his instinct rather
than his generous sympathies for the stowaways? What if he
had said to Emilia, "Flee at once with the children to the

forests outside the city."

"Soon, my love, we'll be together again. God be with you," said Emilia as she embraced him. She took off her chain with its medal of the Virgin and put it around Alfonso's neck. Softly she kissed his lips.

The children sensed his perturbation. Tomás, who rarely cried, began bellowing, and Maruca flung her arms around his waist. "Don't go, Papá," she wept. The children's sobs rang in his ears as he mounted the horse Miguel had procured for him.

Miguel watched all this with a strange, melancholy look.

They clip-clopped along the street. Their bone-thin horses, were too starved to go faster than a slow trot. Outside the City gates they prevailed upon a farmer to sell them a meager measure of hay for 500 *cruzeiros*, nearly all they had.

They journeyed along steep mountain paths to the north. When they arrived at the Count's castle in the evening, Venus was shining in the sky. Dogs barked. Servants lowered a drawbridge over a moat, and their nags ambled across at their leisure.

For a day they were detained because the Count had arranged a special dinner. His aristocratic guests were eager for news of the City. Hungry for intellectual companionship, they engaged Alfonso in lengthy discussions regarding the merits of various Greek and Roman philosophers. It was not until dawn of Easter Sunday that they were able to take their leave. Count Manuel stuffed their purses with 80,000 cruzeiros and provided them with two spirited geldings.

As they rode back, the sun scorched them with unseasonable heat and flies buzzed around them. Late in the afternoon when they approached the Port which bordered the *alfama*, they heard loud voices.

"*Muerte a todos los Judéos.*" They smelled smoke and saw flames flaring up above buildings.

A fat red-haired youth was running down the street. Perspiration dripped down his frightened face. Leaning down over his horse's neck, Miguel grabbed the boy by his hair.

"What's going on?"

"Let me go, Señor"

"Tell us," said Miguel, pulling hard at the boy's hair.

"They say a *converso*, Enrique, mocked the miracle of the Virgin in the Cathedral. Crowds had been gathering to see her smile. He called them all fools and told them it was only the play from a candle near her altar."

The youth's head was at a painful angle. His lips quivered. "Pray let me go, Señor"

Miguel only gripped him harder. "What did they do to Enrique?"

"Señor, it was horrible. They flung themselves on him. They tore his limbs apart. They even tore out hunks of his flesh with their teeth. . . . Señor, let me go."

Then what?" Miguel asked, finally letting go of the boy's hair, but shaking him by the shoulders.

"They began . . . looking . . . killing New Christians in the *alfama*. Let me go. Please let me go! Señores, you, too, had better get out of here as fast as you can."

At last Miguel released the youth, who had begun to sob in terror, and he ran off as fast as his fat legs would carry him.

Miguel turned towards Alfonso. "I must protect my ship and my passengers. You go home. Then bring your family aboard ship as soon as the crowds have gone away."

Alfonso galloped towards his home. As he rounded a corner, he spied a mob led by friars carrying huge wooden crosses as well as spears. "*KILL THE JEWS! KILL THE JEWS!*" the friars shouted, and the crowd echoed their words.

He leapt off his horse and crouched behind a cart of lemons. Then he noticed a door behind him, and he slipped through into darkness. The place smelled of pickled olives and sardines. He heard loud cries and shrieking voices.

After the mob passed through and the noise had died down, he ventured outside. It was unnaturally quiet. His horse was wandering between stone columns of buildings.

He rode on. By now it was dusk. When he reached his

street in the *alfama*, he found himself alone amidst corpses. Again he dismounted, letting his horse wander off. He tripped over a dismembered hand, a poor, jagged hand, and he didn't dare look at it closely for fear he might recognize it. Bodies were piled on top of each other, horribly mutilated. The grocer's entire family had been slain. Arms and legs were severed like pieces of kindling wood, women's bellies ripped apart. The grocer and his little sons had been castrated.

He found Emilia's black slipper with its brass buckle.

She was moaning, her hands pressed against her intestines. Her skirt was lifted up as far as her belly, which had been ripped wide open, and her legs were spread apart like thin brown wings. Her black pubic hair framed a purple flower of blood between her thighs.

He tore off his shirt into strips and tried to bandage her poor, broken body. He held her in his arms, crying out her name over and over, kissing her face and lips as if his kisses could restore her. But her dark eyes were dimmed of life. She breathed only faintly. "The children," she murmured. "Maruca. Tomás."

He held her for a long time, until his arms grew numb, while he whispered words of love and grief and softly kissed her, as if his kisses could heal. She grasped his hand in her cold, weak one. After a while he realized she was no longer breathing, and her hand was rigid around his.

Gently, so gently, he put her down and freed himself from her death grip. Making one last effort, he breathed into her mouth as he had seen *ensalmadores* do, but it was no use. Already she smelled of death.

Only then did he search for his children. Tomás lay partially underneath Maruca's body, as she had vainly tried to protect her little brother. His penis and left leg had been severed, his face smashed in. As for Maruca, the child with the radiant smile, her skull had been split open like a melon.

He knelt down and prayed for their souls, that they might find peace after their horrible deaths. He prayed until it grew entirely dark. Under the faint light of stars, he took Emilia's tortoise shell comb from her soft dark hair and Maruca's tiny golden bracelet and pressed these objects to his heart. But when he gazed at the mutilated body of his little boy, he lay down on the cobblestones, and wrapped his body around the child's. He stayed that way until dawn.

The next morning, in shock, as if in a dream, with a vacant look in his eyes, he searched out Arturo and Avram and others whom he knew well. Arturo's big house had been burned to rubble. In front of it was a huge pile of corpses, and he could not distinguish Arturo and Dorinda among them.

But towards evening, wandering down an unfamiliar side street, he encountered Avram's head upon a pole. The face already looked dried and shrunken.

For days mangled corpses littered the streets. Swarms of black ravens swooped down, pecking out bits of flesh. A few bony dogs and cats gnawed on the remains.

Then wagons came through with burly men, their faces hidden by scarves, who lifted the corpses and flung them into wagons as if they were sides of meat to take to the New Christian cemetery.

He slept on heaps of garbage, if he slept at all. He sipped only a little brackish water from the well, ate only a few crusts of bread. At times, starving mongrels awakened him with their nips, and he would beat them off, by force of habit, with a cudgel.

O my God, why hast thou forsaken me? Why have you taken those I love? Why do evil men reign supreme? Why does evil conquer virtue, like waves sweeping over a narrow strip of bright sand?

I am rootless, truly neither Christian nor Jew, neither Moor nor Albigensian. Sometimes Christ comes to comfort me. But sometimes He mocks me with His laughter.

In his visions Christ merged into Satan, glowing in an aura of flames. But at other times Christ merged into Father Juan, and as he lay on rubble, Alfonso felt surrounded by a strange fluid kindness. This kindness filled his veins.

At other times Emilia clung to him, a ghostly wraith, making love to him with desperation. His children cried for him to bring them back to life. He kept hearing their sobs, night after night.

One day a blow awakened him. Out of habit, he swung his cudgel. When he opened his eyes and saw they were a group of Christian youths, he swung with such fury that they ran off in fright.

Ragged, barefoot, afflicted by hunger, thirst, cold, rain, and burning sun, he found satisfaction in his bodily pain.

Each day the corpses of those who had died of the plague now raging were hauled off in wagons beyond the city gates, where they were burned. By all rights he should have perished, too. *Why hast Thou condemned me to live?*

Avram laughs, his head impaled on a pole. 'As above, so below,' he hisses.

Susannah's head with its long seaweed tresses sways in the wind on a deserted street in Seville. She merges into Emilia, who clings to him like wind.

Alfonso slept and woke, slept and woke through light and dark, heat and cold. Many weeks passed. One day when he awakened, he looked into the eyes of a mongrel who had been nuzzling him. The dog became his pet, the only creature that bound him to this world.

Other people who had gone mad with grief wandered through the streets. One night a crowd of Jews, their garments rent in mourning, marched and played tambourines and danced their way through the *alfama*. Although they were singing in Hebrew, no one dared lay a hand on them.

The Town Crier proclaimed that King Emmanuel had decreed punishment for the massacres. Hundreds of Dominican priests were hurled into dungeons.

Angels came to Alfonso. They sang him sweet melodies, brought him food and drink, rocked him in their arms.

Emilia merged into Susannah, who sat by a fire weeping,

with her long hair wound around her.

"Come," hissed Miguel.

At first Alfonso resisted, but his mother whispered, "You must go with him." He realized how intensely she wanted him to live. So then he let Miguel lead him on board his ship. Angels hovered over them. Someone bathed and clothed him, gave him pure water to sip. Angels hid themselves in the bodies of seagulls. They flew over the ship all the way to Amsterdam, where they abandoned him.

CHAPTER 16

Amsterdam - November, 1506

As he lay in bed, fits of coughing came over him. Wind banged the shutters of Rabbi Goldschmidt's house. The rabbi's daughter, Rachel, a tall bony young woman, changed the dressing around his genitals. Her hands felt cold.

Three days ago he had been circumcised. The next day, deeply troubled in spirit, he had gone for a long walk in thin summer garments. A sudden rainstorm found him far from home. He came down with chills, fever, and with inflammation of the lungs. Although he was now burning with fever, he didn't care. Let the fever consume him. Let him glide over the edge into death. Then perhaps he would rejoin his loved ones. Ah, but it was difficult to breathe. Emilia was beckoning him. Her lips touched his. The cool breath of her spirit brushed his bones.

The shutters kept banging in the wind.

"Benjamin, you must live," whispered the rabbi's daughter, as if she sensed his thoughts. She always called him by his Hebrew name. "You must live," she repeated. Her voice was firm as she timidly stroked his hair. She was awkward at expressing affection. Her mother had died shortly after her birth, and her father, engrossed in study of *Talmud* and in his synagogue, had shown her little warmth.

Earlier the rabbi and Rafael had debated with Alfonso over the circumcision. "You don't have to go through with this," said Rafael, pouring them each a tumbler of schnapps. "I have not been circumcised." They were in his study, crammed with books. Rafael's house now overflowed with furniture and children. In the years since Alfonso as a boy of

thirteen had last seen him Rafael had grown stout. His beard
was flecked with gray. He and Hannah seemed content with
their lives.

"Marranos are excused from circumcision. In adult
males, it often leads to infection," said the rabbi. "Life is precious. A Jew should not endanger himself in a vain attempt to
do what should have been done at birth." He wiped his lips
with the back of his hand. His beard was greasy, and there
were food spots on his vest. However, an expression of aristocratic disdain, passed over his jowled face. He disapproved of
the lax customs of Marranos.

"I must do this for the peace of my soul," insisted Alfonso.
Let the dice be thrown. Life or death. It was in the hands of
the Divine. The desire for circumcision obsessed him. Only in
this way, he felt, could he overcome the shame of having concealed who he was – the shame of his entire family. Centuries
of deceit hung over them like a dark cloud.

If we had not pretended to be other than who we were –
if we had fled Lisbon – if years ago we had left with all the
others during the Exodus and abandoned our wealth – but
many of those Jews perished.

Maimonides believed in the need to preserve one's life,
even if it meant feigning conversion. Survival for Jews was
precarious, and a needless death was an insult to God.
However, Maimonides had not reckoned with the effects of
concealment over a lifetime.

"You can stay with me while you recover," said the rabbi,
as Alfonso had been sleeping on the floor of Rafael's crowded
dwelling. "I have an extra room. Furthermore, I will guide
your study of *Talmud*."

The surgery took place in November, the Hebrew month
of *Kislev*, in the main room of the rabbi's residence. It was
unseasonably cold that morning, and a wet snow was falling.
"The snow is an omen," whispered Rachel.

"My dear, you've got to leave," said the rabbi. "It's not
suitable for you to watch."

"I want to be here," she insisted. Her voice caught with

emotion. Her aunt Rebecca took Rachel's hand. "Let her stay," murmured the older woman. The rabbi turned his back, in this way silently giving permission.

Half a dozen men wearing white embroidered prayer shawls had gathered around Alfonso, who lay on a long table. Underneath the thin blanket he was naked. Earlier they had given him a potion mixed with strong liquor to induce numbness. The snow melted into rain. Through a small upper pane of leaded glass he could see a fine sheet of rain falling.

He closed his eyes.

The rabbi said a benediction. "Our God who hath sanctified us by His commandment and who hath commanded us to bring Benjamin into the covenant of our Father Abraham, we thank You for this day and implore that he be divinely protected by You."

The Mohel unwrapped his knife from its white linen wrappings. With his tight gray curly hair, he reminded Alfonso of Gallimard, the tutor. The knife cut into him. Despite the narcotic potion, Alfonso felt intense pain. Men had begun chanting, and the sounds of their voices seemed to waft him on wings away from the pain of that knife cutting, cutting, tearing away flesh.

His blood flowed into a porcelain basin. The two women washed his wound and bound it in clean linen. Then a shiver ran through Alfonso, as if from a sudden cool breeze. Emilia's presence brushed against his bones. *Come away with me, my love.*

He could hear rain beating on the roof.

The next day, weak but restless, he felt compelled to walk in the open air. Waves rolled against the shoals of the harbor, which was surrounded by flat lands, marshes, and clustered buildings. Ships were departing to other lands, their sails billowing out in the wind. Some were sailing to distant havens for Jews far to the west: Guyana, Pernambuco, Recife, and other tropical lands. Somewhere in those lands their brother Miguel now dwelt. He hoped never to lay eyes on Miguel again!

A raw wind pierced through his clothing, but he kept on walking, far beyond the harbor, heedless of where the road led. Profound despair assailed him. Despite his circumcision, he did not feel himself to be truly a Jew. He was a man who belonged nowhere among the living.

Emilia's spirit hovered close, tantalizing him by her nearness. How alone he was without her, without his children, without the dear ones of his childhood – father, mother, aunt. As for Rafael, he had become a fat, self-satisfied burgher. He had closed himself off from the sufferings of others.

I will join you, my love. Her slender fingers entwined his. The faint odor of her flesh filled the air. Her salty tears stung his eyes. He stumbled over a wagon wheel lying in the road. Next to it a mangy cat was devouring the entrails of a small animal. Gusts of wind blew against him, making it difficult to walk.

That night the fever began. They wrapped him in unguent-soaked rags to lower his bodily heat, and they covered him with soft eiderdown, but to no avail. His lungs filled with phlegm, and he struggled for breath.

Why was he alive?

The pain was like a flaming rosebush. Bursts of flame shot from the swollen tip up his penis up through his groin and bladder, into the pit of his stomach and up into his chest.

Kind women tended him. They put salve on his circumcision wound and bound it again in clean cloth. When he had trouble breathing, they applied steaming compresses to his chest. They smoothed out the bedding, emptied the chamber pot, and fed him spoonfuls of soup.

A doctor applied leeches to his back and arms. However, they had to turn him over and raise him up when a fit of coughing overcame him.

The next day he was worse.

He dreamed he was lost in Cádiz, but the streets had an unfamiliar quality. He heard the Rabbi reciting the 91st Psalm. Unbearably hot, drenched in sweat, he attempted to throw off his coverings, but other hands pushed them down around him. Then he was sailing on a boat, gliding far far away, when a cry called him back. He looked down on his body beneath him, and he saw Rachel sobbing. He felt her force, like a rope pulling him. With a wrench of anguish, he rejoined his body. He felt so hot, and was drenched in sweat.

Then he felt a cool wind rustle through his body. The wings of death bear me aloft, he thought. If God wills, let me die. Oh let me die and join my loved ones.

Rachel came in late that night and gazed at him with love. Beneath the light of her candle, he was so handsome. There was kindness and suffering in his face. She would give her life for his! Yes, she would. She set down the candle, and from her pocket she drew out a Hebrew amulet on a silver chain. It had been blessed by a rabbi in Safed and who was reputed to be a *tzaddik*, one of the thirty-six holiest men on earth. The amulet had been in her mother's family for generations, and she treasured it. Softly she put it around his neck, hiding it beneath his shirt. "Benjamin, you must live. Benjamin, be strong. May God protect you," she murmured. He opened his eyes a little and looked up at her, then turned away. Her hand trembled as she picked up the candle, and a drop of molten wax fell onto the bedding.

The rabbi's snores sounded faintly from his chamber.

Rachel lit more candles and incense from India. She prayed over Alfonso in Hebrew for a long, long time. Her voice murmured like the waters of a brook rippling over stones, rippling harsh Hebrew sounds of the desert, of dry hot winds. At times he opened his eyes and gazed at her. Her narrow, pale face seemed to change into that of a desert chieftain, emitting invisible fire. The flames licked him with an icy coldness.

When the first cocks crowed in the early hours of morning, Rachel laid her hand on his forehead and gave a cry of joy, for the fever had broken. Tears streamed down her face, which was once again that of an ordinary young woman.

Rachel believed herself ugly. She had a narrow face and a

large nose. Taller than most women, she was bone-thin.
However, she did not realize that her dark eyes were beautiful
and that at times she lit up with inner beauty. While she longed
for love she had never known, she also possessed fortitude.
She had a practical spirit and had proved herself most capa-
ble in managing her father's household.

Now believing him still unconscious, she stooped over him
and kissed his lips. " Benjamin, I love you," she whispered.

But he heard her. Why did she care about him? Why did
it matter whether he lived or died? To die ... to drift off with
Emilia.

"Benjamin, Benjamin," she murmured.

His Hebrew name still sounded unfamiliar to his ears, as
if she were speaking to someone else. The old Alfonso floated.
Benjamin was a sturdier being, an alien self, like a thick green
shoot growing out of the stump of a tree that had been cut
down.

In the days that followed, the kind women hovered over
him. Their Dutch voices created soft slushing sounds. Barely
conscious of their ministrations, he was both in his body and
outside himself, floating above himself while Emilia hovered
just beyond reach. Sometimes she brushed him with her fingers or her lips, and her touch was like a feathery wing.

*Mamá. Papá. Emilia and the child in her womb.
Maruca. Tomás. Carlito. Padre Juan.* At times they all beckoned him at once, a crowd of floating lights who impelled him
to float higher and higher, leaving behind this troubled world.
But Rachel clung to him like tenacious seaweed. She wound
around his limbs and would not let him go.

Once he stopped breathing. Terrified, she said his name
over and over like an incantation, and although he struggled
against the voice, it sucked him back into the world of flat
marsh lands, rough voices, and aching hurt.

He pondered why the Jewish covenant with God required
mutilation of the male body. Maimonides himself had written
that circumcision weakens lust and weakens the male member.

Its principal purpose, he wrote, was to provide a visible bond between Jewish men.

Why had he himself felt compelled to go through this surgical ritual? With sadness, he realized that he could never fully belong to the Jews. However, now that he had been circumcised, he could not return to his former life of Marranism. He had cut off that avenue of escape.

He belonged nowhere.

He was neither Christian nor Jew, Spaniard nor Dutchman.

Smells of garlic and cabbage cooking brought him back to the present.

Footsteps.

Damp.

Cold.

His throat was dry.

From an earthen mug he sipped fluid. The mug was held by one of the kindhearted women who had been watching over him. Her hands were large and plump and warm. Sinking back into the eiderdown, he submerged himself once again in memories of his former life which swarmed through his brain with extraordinary vividness.

Much later he awakened, choking in darkness.

Emilia laughed as her silken hair streamed around him. He caressed her face. He ran his fingers over her breasts and belly and thighs. As another fit of choking overcame him, Emilia turned into Susannah's skull. Wind was banging it against a wall.

"Come to me," called Susannah in the wind.

He tried to run, but he sank into soft dark mire.

He woke up fighting for breath.

The next morning at dawn Rachel's steps sounded against the tile floor. Thinking him asleep, she gazed at him with a tender smile. He opened his eyes and looked directly at her. She blushed.

Daily she bathed him with a sponge dipped in cool water.

"You *can't* die," she whispered in a fervent voice.

Emilia, who was floating just beyond reach, burst into peals of laughter. Her laughter filled the room, filled Rachel's pores until Rachel's face expressed a wantonness not her own. Rachel moved about the room, her hips swaying gently, as if Emilia had descended into her.

Alfonso began sweating. The room swirled as he gasped for breath. Emilia encased in Rachel's body held him close against her bony breasts. He lay motionless, yet his mind was split in two and part of him was licking Rachel's ear, sucking her lips, smoothing her belly and her little mound of thick reddish pubic hair. She wriggled out of her clothes and held him close, gyrating her pelvis against him.

Meanwhile, the other Rachel looked down on him with tenderness and fear. He was pale from lack of sunlight, although his body was hairy. He was so tall that his feet reached beyond the edge of the bed. She wanted to lie down next to him and hold him in her arms.

Voices of children playing on the street came through the shuttered windows. Sunlight gleamed dimly. A spoon that she had been holding dropped to the floor. She picked it up and looked down at him in a daze, as if sensing the images of his delirious dreams.

Beneath the quilt so soft he lay.

From the next room came the sound of the rabbi at prayers, familiar kitchen cooking smells, a fragrance of dried herbs.

Alfonso slept and waited.

Slept and waited.

Dawn.

Darkness.

Slowly time passed.

Days and nights flowed into one another.

One day at the market Rachel came upon a peddler with a guitar from Verona for sale. It was very old. The wood was stained and it had no strings, but the peddler produced a packet of cow gut strings. He sold her the guitar for three guilders, and she brought it back to Alfonso, as he said that upon occasion he had played the instrument.

He thanked her, kissing her hands.

Then he strung the instrument, tuned it, and fingered chords awkwardly at first, then with greater ease. He played an Andalusian melody that he remembered from childhood. He fingered a few gypsy melodies as well. Playing the guitar soothed him and brought him back part of the world he had lost.

When he played songs that Emilia used to sing, Alfonso would often feel her presence in the cold, dimly lit room. Invisible to others, she might sit behind them, her hands folded demurely as she mimicked the Dutch women. Then she might float up to the ceiling and gaze down on them all with a mocking smile.

Occasionally she would fly out the window, flapping her arm-wings, to return perhaps with a small fish or bit of garbage clutched between her beak-like lips.

At night she would come into his bed, fragrant with musk and jasmine. But her ghostly embrace could not warm him.

It had grown so cold.

Cold seeped through the eiderdown, numbing him.

Voices around him faded to murmurs, like the humming of insects.

He dreamed that his brother Miguel, grown plump, and Rafael were seated with him at a table in a tavern. Outside the wind blew, and rain beat against the roof, walls, and oiled paper window panes. They were playing at draughts. "The winner will bed Emilia," declared Miguel.

Emilia emerged from behind a Venetian screen. Barefoot, wearing a scarlet dress, she laughed brazenly and waved a fan in front of her face, concealing and then revealing herself. She slipped off her dress. Naked, she sat cross-legged on top of the table, as Alfonso and his brothers continued playing.

One day as Rachel smoothed the bedding, her hand

grazed his newly healed member, causing it to swell in excita-
tion. Quickly Rachel pulled away, blushing.

Alfonso gazed into her eyes. "Could you love me,
Rachel?" a demon in him asked.

Her mouth quivered. She fled from the room.

Over the following weeks he grew stronger. He took long
walks along the canals. Between himself and others he felt a
great distance, as if he were looking at them from far away.
Where would he go? What would he do with the rest of his life?

On those walks Rachel sometimes accompanied him. In
the pale northern sunlight, she looked like a blanched vegetable. However, there was something fiery beneath her bony,
plain appearance, beneath those surprisingly strong muscles
with which she had shifted him when he was bedridden, so that
she could sponge him off or change the linen. In the Dutch
manner, she wore clothing of dark coarse material. Her hair
was demurely covered with a starched white headdress.

He began working again as an accountant, this time for
Rafael in the trading company their father had established
long ago. Several of their ships had *Marrano* crews. In the
hold of these ships, hidden amidst bales and boxes of tin, copper, gold, silver, olive oil, almonds, veils from India, fine linen
from Persia, oranges from Spain, were quarters which shel-
tered *Marrano* families who were fleeing Portugal and Spain.
They reminded Alfonso of Miguel's ship and its ill-fated
arrival in Lisbon a year ago. His brother was now far away in
Recife, an outpost of red brazil trees in the New World.

Alfonso would walk through the crowded streets of
Amsterdam, along canals astir with boats, along the salt
marshes, and by the harbor, crowded with sailing vessels. Flat
lands faded into mists. Smells of fish and sea. These people –
from whom he felt separated by an invisible wall – had a
northern smell, thick and beery, a strong sour pickle smell,
Flemish earth, air, water sweating from their pores.

Smells of salt water, herring, tar.

Taverns along the waterfront welcomed sailors from all

over the world. In these taverns men of different colored skins spoke in various tongues.

Tall narrow stone buildings. Laundry fluttered in damp, icy winds. Peddlers hawked fish and cakes and ale. Ghosts reached out through the bracing wind. Alfonso's parents, hideously scarred by torture, reached out to him. But they were invisible to Rafael, who was walking at his side. Don Carlos laid a hand on Alfonso's, who watched the edges of his father's fingers crumble into black powder. At first his mother was only a smile, soft and tender.

Alfonso, come with us, they begged.

At times his heart would stop for an instant because a woman who sold stockings or bread or who held an infant in her arms resembled Emilia, with her small, graceful body, her gestures, her profile, or her flashing eyes. But when Alfonso approached closer, he would gaze into the face of a stranger.

Each time he felt stricken anew.

Rabbi Goldschmidt, true to his word, had begun to guide Alfonso in studying *Talmud*. A more imaginative and mystically inclined teacher might have drawn Alfonso closer to the spirit of Judaism. However, the rabbi's legalistic approach set Alfonso on edge. Rabbi Goldschmidt focused on countless rules and prohibitions. To Alfonso's way of thinking, the rabbi was a Pharisee who lacked the gifts of wisdom and discernment.

The rabbi slurped his soup, ate with his mouth open, and wiped away pus from his nose onto his beard. His coarse *Ashkenazi* habits repelled Alfonso. He imagined that other *Ashkenazi* men like the rabbi were rude in their intimacies with women. As for the latter, they lacked the grace of their Mediterranean sisters. And what a quantity of drink these northern Jews could consume, until they stumbled over their own feet and acted like buffoons.

The young Spaniard sought clarity by comparing Hebrew beliefs with those of classical Greece. One morning, overcome by gloomy thoughts, he began to read *Phaedo*, which he had

obtained in a well-worn edition from a bookseller. This is the
tract in which Socrates speaks out against dying by one's own
hand. As he sat reading in the main room, Rabbi Goldschmidt
looked over his shoulder. The words were incomprehensible to
the rabbi, as he had never studied Greek.

"You shouldn't read this rubbish!" he cried. "I would not
allow a son of my own to read this barbaric material."

"A fine thing," Alfonso replied. "Ignorance is not a
virtue. Do you know the contents of the material you con-
demn?"

"On the contrary, I honor God by studying His cre-
ations."

"You have lost your faith!" shouted the rabbi, leaping
towards Alfonso. "You Marranos are deceitful to the core. You
accepted baptism with cowardly, false hearts. My own people
slaughtered each other rather than be defiled by baptism.
They threw their children into the Rhine to save them from
Gentiles."

He stood close to Alfonso, breathing hard. Spittle glistened on his rabbi's lips. His heavily jowled face was bright
red with emotion. "Before my time, even when their persecutors held swords at their throats, the Jews of my village taunted them. '*Your Holy Virgin is a whore, the wanton, menstruating mother of a false messiah!*' they would cry."

Alfonso wanted to weep for the rabbi and for the Jews
who had gone with such foolhardy heroism to their deaths. At
the same time, their unyielding rigidity repelled him. In the
sun and warmth of Andalusia, Jews, Moors, and Christians
mingled for centuries, until the Inquisition spread its dragon
wings. However, in cold northern lands Jews stood out as an
alien race among yellow-haired barbarians.

"Our people preferred life to death. Maimonides himself
believed a man should convert if his life were in danger."

"Maimonides was a demon!" shouted rabbi. "I won't
allow his writings inside my house."

"Then I'd better leave," said Alfonso quietly. "I revere

his thought."

At this moment Rachel burst into the room. Evidently she had been listening. Her face was red. "Oh Father! Alfonso! Don't fight! Father, I beg you, let Alfonso read what he wants."

"No, I will leave," said Alfonso. But when he looked at her face, her anguish moved him. He owed his life to her. More than that, to her he owed his will to live. Strong, deep bonds connected them. *"Whom God has joined, let no man put asunder,"* ran through his mind.

Trembling, he went upstairs to his room to pack. Rachel followed him. In the hallway, he turned and gripped her hands. "We'll be together again," he said in a low voice.

"Do you promise?"

"Yes," he said, unable to speak otherwise when he looked into her eyes. He kissed her on the cheek, as a brother would. "I'll be back for you, I promise."

CHAPTER 17

He boarded a ship bound for the northern coast of Spain. consumed by a mad desire to see his country once more, even if it cost him his life. He wanted to travel all through the land, as if in this way he could claim it for his own.

It was the season of storms, and the sea was very rough. Near Gijon, a sleek caravel bore down on them, sailing before the wind. Only a pirate ship would attempt to overtake them in this way. As it neared, sailors lit a fire in an iron pot on the rear deck, next to which they stacked newly made fagots. By now, the pirates' arrows were flying through the air, falling in the water only a few yards short of their vessel. Alfonso dipped a fagot in a barrel of oil, lit it and hurled it through the air. He let fly another and another, until the pirates' mainsail burst into flames.

A cheer sounded from the crew. When they reached the harbor of Gijon the next morning, the grateful captain gave him a purse filled with gold doubloons.

Alfonso purchased a steady-gaited mare and traveled south. It was the month of May, and the land was fresh and green. Although he was beginning his land journey under propitious circumstances, he suffered dreams that caused him to awaken bathed in a sweat of terror.

One night at a roadside inn, when they served roast pork at supper, he had an ominous sense of having dreamed about this very room, these very same strangers. He ate the pork in order not to arouse suspicion. However, a red-bearded man with fair skin called Felix refused the meat.

Later that night, feeling sick from the pork, Alfonso crawled out over the limbs of fellow travelers sleeping in the

large bed and went outside to vomit. Then he started back
towards the inn in search of wine or stronger spirits to kill the
sickness in his belly from the rotten meat.

As he walked, he gazed at the fields which glowed with a
silvery sheen in the moonlight. How beautiful they were. He
wept, thinking of all that he had lost. Overcome with emotion,
he knelt down and kissed the earth. This was his native land,
which he could no longer tread except in Christian disguise.
He wanted to tear the cross form his neck, trample upon it,
and shout out the *Shema*.

*Let them burn him at the stake, roasting him as slowly as
a suckling pig, let them tear out his flesh with pincers. He was
sick to death of concealing who he was, of eating unclean food
and following unclean customs. The disguise was eating into
his soul.*

There are mysterious laws of attraction. The tiniest action
or thought creates endless ripples along the chain of being.
What happened next was no accident but only a portion of the
pattern created by the threads of existence.

At the threshold of the kitchen he stopped, listening to the
scurrying of mice in the darkness. Beneath a closed door
seeped light. Unthinking, he pushed it open. There sat Felix
who was writing on parchment by the light of a candle. Felix
quickly covered the parchment with his hand when Alfonso
walked in, but not before Alfonso had glimpsed Hebrew letters. "*Shalom*," Alfonso murmured. The gold cross around his
neck burned into him, just as it had when he was a small child
down by the docks of Cádiz and he had met the old Jew, and
all the Jews were swarming onto ships.

Felix gazed at Alfonso coldly. With his sharp features he
seemed like a bird of prey.

"*Shalom*, my friend." repeated Alfonso. As if under a
spell, he seized the parchment and gazed at the Hebrew words.
"*May my prayer now, Oh Lord, find favor before You. In Your
great love, Oh God, shield me.*"

Felix stroked his palms together nervously.

"Don't be afraid of me," whispered Alfonso. "I'm no *informante*, but I share your faith. I went outside to empty my belly because the pork made me ill. Come and walk with me in the moonlight."

Felix extinguished the candle with his fingers, stuffed the parchment papers inside his doublet, and silently followed Alfonso into the fields, fragrant with spring vegetation. The dull murmur of a brook assailed their ears. All else was quiet.

"Kabbalists speak of the tree of life," said Alfonso. "We're all part of the tree, which is infinite. Each action ripples endlessly through the world."

The sound of water running over stones grew louder. An owl flew in front of them, then disappeared from view.

" Whether or not you are an informer or an ally, my work is that of the Blessed Holy One," said Felix. He stopped. There was a slight rustling noise, as of branches being trampled. They both trembled. A deer emerged from a clump of bushes. It gazed at them for a moment – all three of them absolutely still – then it took off in graceful leaps.

"*Baruch Atah Adonai*," murmured Alfonso. "May the Lord protect us."

They continued walking until they reached the edge of a wooded copse. There they seated themselves beneath a thick oak tree, and they talked in low voices long into the night of their past lives. Felix told of how he had fled Madrid and of the terrible *auto da fé* that had taken place there, in which hundreds of *conversos* burned. Those who recanted at the last moment were granted the privilege of being strangled on the spot.

In the morning they set off together on the road south towards Léon. Dusk found them far from any inns. So they tethered their horses near a stream, fed them with oats, and built a fire with Felix's tinderbox to keep themselves warm as well as to keep away wolves. They shared a jug of country wine, goat cheese, and hard bread.

Afterwards they sang songs familiar to them both, among

them one that Emilia used to sing:

> *"In the sea there is a tower.*
> *In the tower is a girl*
> *Who calls out to passing sailors*
> *Open your window, oh my dove."*

   The song brought back different memories to both men, as they sat quietly in front of the fire, watching its glow. One of their horses whinnied. They heard what sounded like a small wild creature scurrying through the underbrush. Then all was quiet again. The moon's glow seemed to intensify, illuminating Felix' face.

   From inside his doublet Felix took out a packet of papers, all filled with Hebrew writing. "These are poems and prayers I have written over many years. They are for the Akashic records, which survive forever in the heavens, invisible only to human eyes." For a moment he closed his eyes in contemplation.

   Then calmly he began to toss the parchment papers into the fire.

   "Stop!" Alfonso tried in vain to wrest the papers from him, but Felix tossed the rest into the midst of the flames, which leapt higher.

   "You are mad!" cried Alfonso.

   "No, not at all," said Felix. "These writings are not for other people's eyes. They are for God alone."

   "What were you writing?"

   Felix stared transfixed at the flames that were transforming his parchments into ash. "We're surrounded by evil," he said, pondering his words. "Satan moves among us. We must be ever vigilant. I write truth for the Akashic Records. It doesn't matter if any mortal reads what I write, because the written word takes on sacred power. I write out the messages of spirits. Jehovah and the Archangels hear my voice. As you know, the *Kabbala* teaches that nothing we say or do is ever lost. The Akashic Records retain every word, every action, and every breath."

An animal rustled in the grass. The fire crackled, fanned by a gust of wind.

Alfonso was struck by the other man's faith. While he admired the concept of Akashic Records, he was no longer certain they existed. Nor did he believe in the certainty of a God. Even his earlier visions of Christ, which he had embraced so ardently as a child, he now doubted. The worm of skepticism had burrowed deep inside him. Skepticism, he reflected, was the result of many years of adopting false facades.

A chameleon wriggled out the grass onto bare dirt. Gradually its color changed from grayish green to the color of the earth, fading from Alfonso's view. Like the chameleon, he changed according to his surroundings, to save his life among Christians. But what was his true color? What was a chameleon's? Who did he believe? What did he believe? Were those ecstatic visions of his childhood real, or had they originated in fear? Perhaps as Father Juan had cautioned, they were truly the product of Satan.

"I broke down under torture," Felix said in a low voice. "I wonder if you too have betrayed others."

Alfonso's throat constricted. He could not speak or even breathe.

Ever since his imprisonment there had been something he concealed from himself. While he told himself that he had not betrayed anyone, a tiny merciless voice now rang inside his head. What of the time he been delirious with pain. When he regained consciousness, Inquisitors, like huge black birds of prey, were kneeling over him. They were listening to him intently. He had told himself then that they were wondering if he still lived. But now the realization that they had been listening for his confessions flooded him with shame and horror.

"Jehovah remembers every breath, every impulse, every word. Perhaps in a thousand years people will be ripe to understand what I write." Felix looked into the other man's stricken face. "Yes, you too suffer because you betrayed," he said in a voice filled with compassion.

They parted at Léon. Felix took the mountainous road south towards Salamanca, while Alfonso guided his mare through rich farmlands, hills, and meadows southeast towards Valladolid. As he journeyed on, the land grew drier and the hills became steeper.

A few days later, while he rested in the shade of a cedar tree, his horse tethered nearby, he was roused by the sound of hoof beats. A rider in old-fashioned armor galloped past. Then came an elegant gilded carriage with royal insignia, led by two white horses. One of the rear wheels began to wobble. As it came loose, the carriage swerved and fell into a ditch, landing on its side.

Alfonso ran up to the carriage. He managed to open a door. A disheveled woman of middle years with dark gray hair peered out. She extended her hand, whereupon he helped her get out and lifted her onto the ground. She emanated an overpowering, vile stench. Then he helped a pale blonde younger woman leave the carriage. She appeared to be the other's attendant, and she had a crafty look about her.

The older woman thanked him in a soft but clear voice. "I am Juana, she said. "I am the Queen of Spain." Her mouth quivered, as if she were on the verge of sobbing.

By this time they were flanked by a crowd of attendants. *Juana la loca*, someone murmured. All Spain had heard of *Juana la loca*, the madwoman who was the rightful successor to Isabel and Ferdinand. Juana drew herself up with dignity.

"I'm in your debt, Señor."

"No, Your Highness. It is I who am indebted for the honor of helping you," said Alfonso, bowing so low that his black leather hat scraped the dusty road. He was outraged at the murmurings of her courtiers, and he sensed that she possessed a true, if wounded nobility of spirit.

The queen's eyes were dark and gentle, set in a careworn face. Despite the richness of her dress, there was a tear in the hem of her black velvet skirt, and there were stains on the black silk bodice. A heavy golden cross dangled between her breasts. Her hair was swept up awkwardly, with thick strands escaping along her shoulders.

He had heard tales of how she married Felipe of Flanders for love. He had heard of her jealousy over his faithlessness, of how he died in Flemish lands, and of how she journeyed to the north to retrieve his corpse, which she transported through all of Spain.

Peasants felt that she had been deeply wronged, that she had been driven to madness through the cruelty of others. They said that on the few occasions when she had given speeches, she moved people by her clarity and sense of justice. She had captured their hearts, and the common people considered her almost a saint.

Pray for me. They say I am mad. Sometimes, however, my mind is as lucid as water from a mountain spring. I was starved for love, in a way that only young girls can be when their bodies cry out for seed.

Felipe repaid my love, after I had borne him eight children, by locking me up in the castle at Valladolid. Now my eldest son keeps me a prisoner there, too, so that I will not interfere with his rule of Spain, this son of mine who does not even speak Castilian, who was raised too far from me, and who has no love for me in his heart.

In truth, I neglected him as I traipsed after his wandering father, following him with his soldiers to Flanders and back to Spain again.

Father and son both played me false.

Only my youngest, Nina, loves me.

From my windows at Valladolid, dulled with dirt and grime, I watch the river flow in the distance.

Constantly I urinate.

For entire days and nights, I may not be conscious of my body or surroundings, and I may awaken to find myself lying in my own filth. But my body and the room seem as distant as if they were in a dream, while my spirit, a bright flame, flickers above the huddled body on the bed. Courtiers scurry around to clean up the mess. I weep invisible tears; I smile with invisible tenderness for my wretched body.

My lady-in-waiting, the Countess Liliana, holds a scented vial to her nose as she approaches the bed. With the help of two maidservants, she strips me bare to the waist and sponges my sunken breasts and distended belly with cool seawater. They wrap cloths around me, draping me from public view as they strip me below the waist, and from an enormous distance I feel the sponge wash over my feet and ankles, legs, and thighs, and feel the sponge against my female parts. They turn me over to wash my buttocks, emitting cries of disgust. "How she stinks!"

I smile and weep inaudibly.

Later they wrap me in a velvet robe and place me in a chair by the window. I watch the afternoon turn to dusk, watch the river grow dark, watch wind blow the branches of pine and oak and olive trees. A bird flies close to the casement window. Mistaking the smoky glass for an opening, the bird nearly brushes its wings against me.

"Pray over his corpse," the Cardinal told me in secret. "Miracles have occurred when the dead awaken through the power of prayer."

So I took his corpse in a mahogany casket to sacred places all through Spain, to cathedrals as well as to modest chapels which had been the site of appearances of the Virgin.

I fasted and prayed.

God did not grant my prayers.

Felipe never awakened.

Now they have buried his body in a far-off crypt.

Sometimes I hear his voice in my dreams, and he laughs lovingly, as he never did in life. He holds me with more ten-

derness than he ever did before.

"Señor, oh I wish that you could take me away with you," she said abruptly.

Alfonso was not sure he had heard her correctly, so unexpected were her words. However, he replied, "Your Majesty, I wish it were in my power."

A bitter smile flickered over her features. "I'm not 'your Majesty'. In truth, I am a prisoner. These people are not my servants but my jailers, and they're trying to poison me. I beg you, take me to my daughter. They've taken away Nina, my youngest and dearest. My only friend. Take me to her." The queen's eyes filled with tears. Despite her pathetic situation and ravaged appearance, he thought there was majesty about her.

"I wish I could, your Majesty. But your servants wouldn't permit it."

"I'm shut up all day in my rooms without a soul to talk to except servants hired by my son or my father, Ferdinand, who spy on me. If I don't behave according to their wishes, they won't even allow me to open the curtains and look out at the sky."

"How then did you get out today in your coach?"

"I'm only allowed out to go to Mass. I asked permission to make a special pilgrimage to the shrine of Saint Caterina. For months I've begged to go. While I'm gone, even now perhaps my nobly born attendants are searching through my personal effects. Now that they've deprived me of my daughter, they're stealing my books, my letters, my jewels. Oh take me away from all this!"

The queen clasped his right hand in both of hers. They felt cold, despite the heat of the day. "Nina used to run down to the kitchen and bring me back pure, unpoisoned food. We fed the food that the servants had prepared for me to my pet spaniel and, after three months of their diet, my darling died. Oh, take me away from here! Countess Liliana drugs my food, so I refuse to eat." Juana gestured to her golden-haired lady-in-waiting, who gave him a brief look of complicity.

"Help me please, Señor," the queen begged.

"My Majesty, I will pray for you," said Alfonso. He felt weak in his knees, overcome with the pathos of this woman's situation. "May God's grace be with you."

He bowed low again, once more scraping the dust of the road with his hat.

The queen looked down at her hands. Her jagged fingernails were rimmed with dirt. She slid an ornate gold and emerald ring from her skinny middle finger. "Remember me, Señor," she said, offering it to him.

Alfonso cradled the ring in his hand and kissed it. "Your Majesty, I'm greatly honored."

Countess Liliana clutched the queen's sleeve. "We must go," she said.

An oily-faced footman helped her into the carriage, which the attendants had lifted from the ditch. The footman winked at Alfonso as the coachman flicked his whip over the horses' rumps, and the procession moved on.

A fortnight later Alfonso was in Cádiz, disguised as a beggar. He wore a wig, false eyebrows and false beard purchased from a traveling troupe of actors in the north. With slow steps, saying his beads, he walked along familiar streets. He didn't recognize anyone, except for the old, hunchbacked fishwoman who still peddled her wares on a corner near the main plaza.

As he approached the tall iron gates of his former home, he held his breath. Above the stone walls, the house loomed over adjacent buildings. It looked the same at first. However, as he came closer, he realized that wrought iron bars over the lower windows had been replaced by closed shutters. The flowering jasmine plants that crept up along the balconies had vanished.

A Dominican monk in his black robes approached. Alfonso sank into the shadows of a nearby building and watched him open the gate with a large key. With a start, he realized that this monk had been a childhood friend. As boys they had occasionally played together.

More Dominican clergy entered through the gates. Their house had become a monastery. It harbored monks, Inquisitors, and *familiares*.

He crouched against the shadows, willing himself to be invisible, although he longed to shout out, "This is my house!" He restrained an impulse to draw his sword from its sheath beneath his beggar's robe.

Instead, he stayed hidden, concealed by a flowering lemon tree as the shadows lengthened. The sun set. Stars appeared. Under the night sky he contemplated the home where his family had lived for generations, and he tried to absorb it through his pores. He knew he would never lay eyes on it again. It grew cold. He shivered in his rags.

Then he stole away.

Shortly after dawn, mingling with a crowd of beggars and artisans, he passed unnoticed through the city gates.

CHAPTER 18

Not long after Alfonso returned to Amsterdam, on a warm afternoon in July, he and Rachel were married in the synagogue. The men dressed in heavy black suits, despite the heat. The women wore pale silk summery gowns. Rachel's father officiated as rabbi. While Rabbi Goldschmidt spoke the Hebrew words that would bind them together for life, Alfonso glanced at Rachel. Meeting his eyes, she flushed behind her veil. She wore a white silk gown and a tall headdress embroidered with pearls. Her fingers trembled when he slid on the gold ring, and he felt a mournful heaviness. Despite the heat, her hands were cold. But afterwards they quickly warmed when he took her in his arms and danced with her.

People feasted and danced until daybreak to the music of a flute, a lyre, and two guitars, while children and old ones fell asleep, laying their heads down on the tables, curling up on the floor of the great hall in which the festivities were being held, or sleeping outside in the courtyard.

Hours earlier Alfonso and Rachel had entered the bridal chamber. Passive and frightened, she let him remove her clothing before he removed his own. She shivered as they stood before each other in the candlelight. Then he took her in his arms and half carried her to the bed. Her head had been closely shaven, according to Ashkenazi custom, and this shocked him. She looked so pathetic without the chestnut hair that had once hung to her waist. He wanted to comfort her for her plainness, her flat breasts, her long, ungainly limbs. Yet at the same time he found these features strangely arousing. When he mounted her, she lay very still beneath him. Her membrane was thick. He pounded against it. She muffled cries of pain, clenching her lips.

Then at last he broke through, and she bled so copiously he feared he had injured her.

He put a linen cloth between her thighs to stop the blood from flowing, and he held her close. She lay almost unmoving, allowing his fingers to roam over her soft skin.

"Do you truly love me?" she asked.

"Yes," he said, clearing the phlegm that suddenly blocked his throat. But in his mind, Emilia's limbs twined around his; her voice whispered in his ear; her long-vanished scent filled his nostrils.

Three months later the young couple sailed for Recife and the promise of a better life. Miguel had settled there with a few other Sephardic families. He wrote that in this lush tropical land one could gain a fortune from the reddish-hued brazil wood, which was prized for its beauty. Furthermore, people talked of gold in the mountains.

Before their marriage, Rachel and Alfonso had discussed the idea thoroughly. Rachel believed that they and their descendants would fare better on this new, unexplored continent, far from the Inquisition. Finally, despite his intense aversion for Miguel, Alfonso decided to go.

On the Canary Islands their ship picked up African slaves, who were chained beneath in the hold. Their cries and moans were most piteous. And it was horrible to see the corpses of those who had died thrown overboard. Sharks followed in their wake, hungry for those bodies so cruelly deprived of life. A few days further out at sea, gulls that had been circling over their ship and diving for morsels of food turned back to shore.

As they approached the Equator, the stars grew larger and more brilliant, the air softer. The languid breezes (for they were on a fortunate course) brought out musicians among the sailors and passengers. At night the strum of guitars and mandolins and the beat of drums filled the air.

Brilliant parrots with red and green and gold feathers were teased ferociously by the monkeys that clambered over the ship.

There were a few goats and chickens. Animals, people, music all mingled.

Late one afternoon, when the wind had risen higher than usual, Rachel walked towards Alfonso on the forward deck, her body swaying with the movement of the ship. He patted her slightly rounding belly. For two months she had not menstruated. The severity of her white headdress suddenly angered him because it seemed so much at odds with the natural flow of her body. Sephardic women did not shave their heads upon marrying. They did not hide their beauty.

Her shorn head had bothered him from the very first night of their marriage, and now this mutilation of her sensuality, symbolized by her headdress and her shorn hair, aroused in him a boiling anger. He tore off the kerchief and flung it over the railing into the sea. She shrieked, clasping her hands over her head.

"Grow your hair!" he said. "No more kerchiefs! I want you to be a woman! Not a nun!"

"No!" she screamed.

"Only Ashkenazi women cut their hair. I want you to grow it long. I want you to be beautiful for me!"

Sobbing, she flung herself into his arms, burying her head in his shoulder to hide its bareness.

"The Talmud . . ."

"The Talmud does not command you to mutilate your hair. Only the Ashkenazi shear their women like sheep."

She ran down to their tiny cabin, locked the door, and sobbed until she fell asleep many hours later, curled up on the floor beneath their berth. For three days she did not eat.

For his part, he was furious with her. He slept on the deck and avoided her.

The other passengers began to speak about them, some with hushed voices, others with raucous laughter.

For three days Rachel locked herself in their cabin. On the third morning she emerged, pale, haggard, in a new blue and white headdress, holding herself like injured royalty. She walked up to Alfonso. He embraced her tightly. She whispered in his ear, "I want to please you. I want to be beautiful for you."

As they walked hand in hand, she murmured, "Ruth followed her husband to a new land, and she followed the customs
of his people. I will follow yours, and I'll let my hair grow long
as I did when I was a girl."

In their narrow berth at night, with renewed ardor they
gave pleasure to each other. "Teach me how to be wanton," she
murmured. He guided her torso and her thighs, rotated her hips
in lascivious movements that were foreign to her rigid upbring-
ing. He invented erotic games, in which he was the master and
she a slave. Then he would demand that they reverse roles. She
went along with all this to please him.

But in the mornings when she was alone, after Alfonso had
gone above to the deck, she would chant her prayers in Hebrew,
imploring the Blessed One for forgiveness, swaying back and
forth on her prayer cushion.

One night when she had fallen sound asleep after their
bouts of ardor, he restlessly strolled the deck. The moon was full.
He heard the strains of a Ladino melody. At first he thought he
was imagining things, thought perhaps the sound was only an
illusion wrought by the wind and his longing. However, the
music grew louder.

> *"In the sea there is a tower*
> *In the tower is a window*
> *In the window is a girl*
> *Whom the sailors call…"*

A crowd of men were gathered together on the stern deck
beneath the shrouds. The first mate, who had once sailed with
Vasco da Gama, was leading in a lusty voice, while he strummed
a guitar. A tall, thin passenger accompanied with a flute.

"*Shalom!*" shouted a sailor. "*Shalom!*" roared the others
in response.

Exultation filled his heart so that he thought he would burst with joy. The full moon bathed them in glittering silver light. On the shore, tropical birds slept in the shadows of dunes. However, a few restless gulls, perhaps drawn by memories of a distant past, soared over their ship, accompanying them through the night sky as a favorable wind speeded them towards the new land.

Epilogue

The *Kabbala* teaches that God marks out the paths of our
lives before we are born. One wonders. So many lives
have been torn, like limbs from a tree split by lightning. Does
He truly wish us well, or does He contain a malignant streak?

The intense heat, disease, and primitive conditions in
which they lived during those early years in Recife made the
settlers' lives precarious. Three of Alfonso's and Rachel's children died in infancy. What raised the couple's spirits and gave
them strength to endure was that for many years virtually all
the families in their small colony were Marranos. The settlers
built a whitewashed church, which they called the Chapel of
Our Lady of Mercy in order to keep up appearances for occasional outside visitors. However, it was in reality a synagogue.
If strangers were present, the priest conducted services in
Latin. But when the settlers were alone, he led them in worship of a Hebrew god.

In this land Alfonso built a fortune.

He was one of the first to carve out a sugar plantation on
the fertile land, where the cane grew with almost magical
abundance. North of the town, along the banks of a muddy
river he cleared fields and planted them with cane. For his
large family, he built a mansion. Rachel managed the household with her characteristic energy. As their riches increased,
he hired tutors for their children and surrounded them with
luxuries.

In this land the colors were more brilliant and the heat
more intense than even in the south of Spain. There was a delicious softness in the humid air, and among the natives a childlike innocence with matters of the flesh. Along with the languid

heat there existed an inner music in the atmosphere. Laxity reigned during those early years of colonization, increased by the sweetness of gold pressed into greedy palms. The Inquisition had not yet dug in its talons, and during this time Jews barely bothered to disguise who they were. Officials and commoners alike shared a scoffing devil-may-care attitude towards any ecclesiastic authority.

In this seductive land, Kabbalistic teachings gradually lost their appeal for Alfonso, as more worldly pleasures grasped him. Old convictions fell away, like dead fronds from a palm tree.

However, as Rachel approached middle age, she became more rigid in her observance of the rituals with which she had grown up. The kosher dishes that had come with them from Holland were taken out of storage, and she taught the servants to cook food in the old ways of her people. She cropped her gray hair and resumed wearing her former Ashkenazi head-dress.

Traders were bringing in ever greater numbers of slaves from Africa. These dark-skinned people were stronger and better adopted to the land than the natives, who clung to jungle shade. Gradually, slaves replaced their Indian workers. Rachel was unhappy with the idea of their owning slaves, but Alfonso brushed her protests aside, as their labor greatly profited him.

Wizened and thin, dried out by the heat, with her shorn locks, Rachel ceased bearing children. Physical attraction between her and Alfonso had long ago died. Alfonso sought to satisfy his lust with slave girls. Subsequently feeling scruples of conscience, he would then give generous donations to the Benedictines and Augustinians, as both these religious Orders had recently established themselves in the vicinity. He gave funds for the building of a large church in Recife as well as gold to the semi-secret Hebrew charity for the poor.

Saddened and angered by his unfaithfulness, Rachel moved into a separate suite of rooms. She spent many hours in prayer. With age, she began to resemble her father in the narrowness of her outlook on life.

However, she continued to manage the household and servants with admirable efficiency, and she found outlet for her energy in charitable work. When cholera broke out, she nursed the sick, including their own slaves, with devotion. Miguel, who still captained a ship, had the misfortune to land during the cholera outbreak, and he died of the fever. Thereupon Rachel insisted on taking his children and his widow into their household.

Occasionally Rachel would encounter a slave child with Alfonso's features. Then she would feel a rush of sadness and tenderness for this creature, sprung from the seed of the man she had once loved so much.

She died in her sleep at the age of fifty-three. Slaves, children, and grandchildren, all mourned her death. Their plantation slaves drummed, danced, and chanted through the night to ease the passing of their mistress into other realms.

After her burial, Alfonso rode off into the jungle, as he craved solitude in which to pray and reflect. Many days later he returned, slumped half-conscious in the saddle, leaning his head against his horse's neck. He was delirious with feverish visions. His youngest son helped him to bed.

When Alfonso recovered, he gave one hundred thousand gold ducats to the town's Hebrew charity. He ordered the servants to continue cooking food in the kosher manner their mistress had showed them. He donned a *tallit* and wound *tefillin* around himself for prayers. He secluded himself in his study, devoting hours each day to study of *Torah* and *Talmud*, and he delegated the work of overseeing the plantation to his sons.

But after a time he felt compelled to return to his duties. And the land gradually regained its hold over him. The languid heat, the music, the beat of slave drums at night, all reawakened his senses. Once again he began to frequent young slave girls.

"Alfonso," murmured Emilia in the soft breeze one day,

as he rode his horse through the green plantation. The Emilia of his youth floated like a wisp in the heat. Her husky voice mingled with the cawing of birds and the rustling of leaves.

He heard a song that made him ache with longing for the past.

> *" In the sea there is a tower,*
> *In the tower is a girl ...*
> *Give me your hand, oh my dove*
> *So I may watch you sweetly sleeping ...."*

He followed the sound to its source. Near the slave huts with their small vegetable patches, a girl in a white dress sat against the trunk of a cassava tree. She strummed a guitar as she sang.

When Alfonso reined in his horse, he looked down into the eyes of a young Emilia with mahogany skin and copper hair. She gazed at him without a trace of fear. Emilia's eyes shone through hers, and she smiled with the young Emilia's brilliant, mischievous smile.

He moved the girl into his house, married her, and lived with her for thirty years until his death.

Today Alfonso's descendants have scattered over the planet. One lives in a Paris attic and writes Third World manifestoes. Another sells women's underwear on a street corner in Rio. Still another is a Cardinal at the Vatican, while his distant cousin is an Orthodox rabbi.

Although Emilia left no earthly children, many of Alfonso's descendants possess her eyes and features, as though her spirit had implanted chromosomes inside their bodies.

Emilia's ghost smiles as she wafts over rooftops.

From a San Francisco nightclub come the refrains of old Sephardic melodies. A young girl with the shining eyes and husky voice of Emilia is singing.

A Note on "Marrano"

It is with great hesitation that I decided to use this word, because "Marrano" is a pejorative term that means "swine." However, it is far more than that. Historically, it refers to hundreds of thousands of Spanish and Portuguese Jews who converted to Christianity in order to survive—often they were forcibly converted—but who continued to practice Judaism in secret. It has been estimated that while approximately 300,000 Jews left Spain in 1492, more than 400,000 remained, weaving themselves into the fabric of Spanish culture. In reaction, the Inquisition gained force. "Marranism" refers to an entire way of living, an entire culture that survived for centuries through the concealment of identity.

In the preface to her fascinating book, *The Mezuzah in the Madonna's Foot*, Trudi Alexy writes: "The drama of the Marranos' dogged determination to cling to their way of life, holding fast to their beliefs and practicing their laws and traditions when being found out meant torture and death, symbolizes, for many, the importance of a connection to one's ancestral roots and the miraculous survival of the spirit, even in the most hostile of environments."

However, such concealment is not without psychological dangers. The ramifications in my own family have continued to reverberate through five centuries. It was the desire to examine these roots that inspired this novel.

GLOSSARY

Alfama – Jewish or Moorish quarter. (Portuguese.)

Aljama – Jewish or Moorish quarter. (Spanish.)

Anusim – Forced converts.

Ashkenazim – Jews of central and eastern Europe.

Akashic records – Eternal records of all that has ever happened. The word "Akashic" stems from Sanscrit "akasa", meaning ether or atmosphere.

Aramaic – Semitic language spoken between 300 B.C. and 650 A.D. Its script is the basis of written Hebrew.

Auto da fé – Public sentencing of transgressors, especially heretics, by the Inquisition. They would be handed over to civil authorities for execution.

Av – Eleventh month of the Jewish lunar year.

Compline – Late night. The last of the seven canonical hours, times set aside for prayer and worship.

Converso – Jewish or Moorish convert to Christianity.

Ein sof – The Endless.

Familiares – Officers of the Inquisition.

Juana la Loca – 1479-1555. Daughter of Ferdinand II. and Isabella I.

Kabbala – Body of mystical beliefs developed in Spain in the twelfth century. Its roots are far more ancient, and it has been conjectured that there are connections with Hindu philosophy.

Ladino – Spanish dialect of Sephardic Jews.

Lauds – First canonical hour. Early morning.

Maimonides – 1135-1204 A.D., Major Jewish philosopher, born in Spain.

Marrano – Spanish or Portuguese Christian convert who secretly continued to practice Judaism. Literally, "swine".

Marranism – Social conditions associated existing as a Marrano.

Muezzin – Crier who summons Moslems to prayer.

New Christians – Jewish converts.

Regidor – Member of inner communal council.

Sambenito – Yellow robes of penance prescribed by the Inquisition.

Sephardim – Jews of Spain, Portugal, and North Africa.

Sephirot – The ten emanations of the Divine which permeate the universe.

Sext – Fourth canonical hour. Midday.

Shekhinah – Divine Presence as female, according to Kabbalistic thought.

Susannah la Hermosa – c. 1464-1497. The street in Seville where she died is still known as Calle de la Muerte.

Tallit – Jewish prayer shawl.

Talmud – Collection of Jewish laws and traditions, including interpretations of Torah.

Tefillin – Two leather cubes containing fragments of the Torah attached to leather bindings. They are worn on forehead and forearm by Orthodox Jewish males during prayer.

Terce – Third canonical hour. Mid morning.

Torah – First five books of the Old Testament.

Tzaddik – A fully enlightened being.

ACKNOWLEDGMENTS

Many people have helped me with this story. Barbara Atchison carefully read through several drafts. Her enthusiasm and discerning comments helped me keep on going. Arthur Benveniste, Lucha Corpi, Luba Davis, Molly Dwyer, Lucille Eichgreen, Roberta Fernández, Judy Frankel, Rebecca Fromer, Sally Headding, Sara Levi, Marcelle McCallahan, Paula Nuñes, Victor Perera, Tazz Powers, Esther Sabin, Marc Sabin, Judith Stephens, Nancy Threatt, and Brenda Webster all contributed time, energy, and valuable feedback, as did my brother, Lee Cronbach, and my daughter, Carmen Espinosa. I am grateful for the support of Rhoda Curtis, Helene Knox, and Richard Zimler. My husband, Walter Selig, was proofreader par excellence as well as Hebrew consultant. Dr. Avram Davis of Chochmat HaLev Meditation Center in Berkeley was extremely helpful with concepts of *Kabbala*. Sister Rosario Asturias, professor of Spanish Literature at Holy Names College, Oakland, provided me with valuable information. The late Irving Halperin, professor at San Francisco State University, was a catalyst with his inspiring lectures on Jewish literature. I thank my old friend and former teacher, Nanos Valaoritis, who believed in my writing all these years. I am deeply indebted to my publisher, Bryce Milligan, for his support and his editorial suggestions.

I also want to thank Ragdale Foundation and the Virginia Center for the Creative Arts for providing space and tranquility in which to work.

Finally, my gratitude goes to many others not mentioned whose contributions have been invaluable.

ABOUT THE AUTHOR

Born **Paula Cronbach** to a family of German Jews with hidden Sephardic origins, María Espinosa's family had lived in Spain until the 18th century, hiding their Jewish identity until the family finally made their way to Brussels. Espinosa grew up in Long Island, the child of a sculptor father and a poet mother. She attended Harvard and Columbia Universities and received a MA in Creative Writing from San Francisco State University. She met and married her first husband, Chilean writer Mario Espinosa Wellmann while living in Paris. In 1978 she married Walter Selig, who had fled Nazi Germany as a child to grow up on an Israeli kibbutz.

Espinosa has taught at New College of California and City College of San Franciso. She is the author of two prior novels, *Longing* and *Dark Plums* (both Arte Público Press, 1995). *Longing* has been translated into Greek. Espinosa is also the author of two books of poetry, *Night Music* and *Love Feelings*. She translated George Sand's novel, *Lélia*, which was published by the Indiana University Press.

For a more complete biographical information, Espinosa is included in *Contemporary Authors*, Vol. 30 (Gale Research, 1999).

Colophon

One thousand five hundred copies of the first edition of *Incognito: Journey of a Secret Jew*, by María Espinosa, have been printed on 70 pound non-acidic paper. Titles have been set in Sheer Type, a modified form of Mazel Tov; initial capitals in Caslon Openface Type. The text was set in a contemporary version of Classic Bodoni, originally designed by the 18th century Italian typographer and punchcutter, Giambattista Bodoni, press director for the Duke of Parma.

This book was entirely designed and produced by
Bryce Milligan, publisher, Wings Press.

Wings Press was founded in 1975 by Joanie Whitebird and Joseph F. Lomax as "an informal association of artists and cultural mythologists dedicated to the preservation of the literature of the nation of Texas." The publisher/editor since 1995, Bryce Milligan is honored to carry on and expand that mission to include the finest in multicultural American writing.

Other recent and forthcoming literature from Wings Press

Way of Whiteness by Wendy Barker (2000)

Hook & Bloodline by Chip Dameron (2000)

Splintered Silences by Greta de León (2000)

Incognito: Journey of a Secret Jew by María Espinosa (Fall 2002)

Peace in the Corazón by Victoria García-Zapata (1999)

Street of the Seven Angels by John Howard Griffin (Spring 2003)

Winter Poems from Eagle Pond by Donald Hall (1999)

Initiations in the Abyss by Jim Harter (Fall 2002)

Strong Box Heart by Sheila Sánchez Hatch (2000)

Patterns of Illusion by James Hoggard (Fall 2002)

This Side of Skin by Deborah Paredez (Fall 2002)

Fishlight: A Dream of Childhood by Cecile Pineda (Fall 2001)

The Love Queen of the Amazon by Cecile Pineda (Fall 2001)

Bardo99 by Cecile Pineda (Fall 2002)

Face by Cecile Pineda (Spring 2003)

Smolt by Nicole Pollentier (1999)

Garabato Poems by Virgil Suárez (1999)

Sonnets to Human Beings by Carmen Tafolla (1999)

Sonnets and Salsa by Carmen Tafolla (Fall 2001))

The Laughter of Doves by Frances Marie Treviño (Fall 2001)

Finding Peaches in the Desert by Pam Uschuk (2000)

One Legged Dancer by Pam Uschuk (Fall 2002)

Vida by Alma Luz Villanueva (Spring 2002)